By the Same Author

WHITE CAPTIVES

RATTLESNAKE CAVE

GO UP THE ROAD

(MARGARET K. MCELDERRY BOOKS)

THE POTLATCH FAMILY

THE POTLATCH

A MARGARET K. MCELDERRY BOOK

FAMILY

Evelyn Sibley Lampman

ATHENEUM · New York 1976

Chapter ornament designed by Diane de Groat

LIBRARY OF CONGRESS CATALOGING IN PUBLICATION DATA

Lampman, Evelyn Sibley.   The potlatch family.
"A Margaret K. McElderry book";
Summary: Looked down at by her classmates because
of her darker skin and alcoholic father, a Chinook
Indian girl gains a new outlook when her brother
returns from Vietnam.
[1. Indians of North America—Fiction]   I.   Title
PZ7.L185Pq   [Fic]   75-28328
ISBN 0-689-50039-4

Published simultaneously in Canada by
McClelland & Stewart, Ltd.
Manufactured in the United States of America
by H. Wolff, New York
Designed by Suzanne Haldane
First Edition

THE POTLATCH FAMILY

Mrs. Heacock was hammering on the horn when I came running out of the school door. It surprised me some because I thought Mary Beth Perkins or Wendy Carter would have told her why I was late. They were the only two girls in my P.E. class who took the Cooperville school bus, and I was sure they'd have explained to Mrs. Heacock about Kelley Brennan, but they hadn't. Even Mrs. Heacock would have been impressed by Kelley.

All during the last period we'd wondered why somebody who was on the rally squad and was secretary of the student body and just about the prettiest and most popular girl in the senior class was watching

3

a freshman gym class. I could hear the others whispering about it while Miss Miller put us through our paces. Nobody whispered to me, but I wondered too. You could have knocked me over with a puffball when Miss Miller finally blew her whistle and bellowed, "That's all for today. Everybody for the showers." Then she yelled, "Longor, Brennan here wants to talk to you." Miss Miller always calls everybody by their last names. I don't know why.

You should have heard the buzzing when she said that. It was just like a new swarm of bees around a fresh tree. The kids kept hanging back when I went over, but Kelley Brennan didn't start talking until everybody had gone. I couldn't believe what she was saying, but she understood why I had to say no. Kelley Brennan was nice. I guess people who have everything can afford to be.

The showers were empty when I got there. I figured Mary Beth or Wendy would want to be the first to find out what Kelley wanted but I took my shower just like I always do, with soap. Most of the kids don't bother with soap. They just turn on the water, dash under, turn around and get out. I always scrub real good with the school's soap because we don't have a bathtub at home. Pop keeps promising Mom that he'll put one in some day, but I don't know where he'd put it. Our house is pretty old, and when Mom finally got him to put in an inside toilet, there was only room for that and a wash basin in the closet off the kitchen. You can get clean using a wash basin and a cloth, but it takes a long time. That's why I do such a good job of scrubbing at school, and why I'm glad P.E. is the last period of the day.

"I was going to give you one minute more, Plum Longor," said Mrs. Heacock when I came hurrying up. "Then I was going to drive off and leave you. What'd you have done then?"

"Walk home, I guess, Mrs. Heacock," I said, but I don't know if she heard me because she'd already started up the bus.

I looked down the aisle, half expecting that either Mary Beth or Wendy would have saved me a seat. They never did, but this time I thought maybe their curiosity would have got the better of them. Then I could see they were going to play it cool. They were acting as though Kelley Brennan asking to speak to a strange freshman girl happened every day. I could see them, sitting together, and the other girls that used to go to Cooperville Elementary were all sitting close around, like always.

As usual, there was only one seat left. Half a seat really, because Mildred Schultz took up so much room that she didn't leave much space. I always sat with Mildred Schultz. She was from Cooperville, too, and I'd known her since the first grade. She was an outsider, just like I was. I mean, she wasn't ever invited to parties, and she never had a best friend to eat lunch with or anything. But for different reasons. Mildred was fat and she never wanted to do anything but study. And if you said something to her, like "What time is it?" she'd sit and stare at you for a whole minute before she got around to looking at her wrist watch. But at least she was white, not Indian like me, and her Pop didn't get drunk sometimes and lie down on the street to sleep it off. I squeezed in the little space Mildred had left and braced my feet for the curves.

The girls always sat in the front of the bus and the boys as far back as they could get. Janet Carruthers and Patty Murrow were just behind Mildred and me, but they were turned around talking to the other girls. I wondered if Mary Beth and Wendy had told them about Kelley Brennan wanting to talk to me. They didn't act like it.

"What you reading, Mildred?" I asked. I didn't really care, but it's hard to be quiet when everybody else is talking and jabbering a mile a minute.

Mildred kind of shook her head and put her finger on a word to mark the place. Then she looked over at me with her blue popeyes for a long time before she said, "History." After that she went back to reading.

Mrs. Heacock kept stopping the bus to let kids out at farm roads, and pretty soon she turned off the main highway to the graveled road that led to Cooperville. It was ten miles up in the foothills of the Coast range, and a stiff climb. It's pretty in summer when the wild roses and fox gloves and fireweed are in bloom under the big fir trees, but now it was just wet and soggy. The leaves were off everything but the firs, and muddy rain water filled the ditches on each side. In the hollows, water even crossed the road. It wasn't deep, though, and the bus just plowed right through, sending spray almost up to the windows. We never had any trouble picking out our bus when a lot of

6

them were parked together. The Cooperville bus was always the dirtiest.

Pretty soon I felt someone jabbing me. It was Janet Carruthers.

"Mary Beth says Kelley Brennan wanted to talk to you after P.E. today. What did she want?"

I felt like laughing inside but I didn't let on. Curiosity had finally got the cat. For a minute I felt like saying it was none of her business. But I didn't. I wanted them all to know.

"Nothing much," I told her, trying not to sound too boastful. "She just asked me to try out for freshman rally is all."

"For freshman rally!" Janet squealed so loud that Mildred put her finger on her place and looked up from her book. "You?"

"Yes, me." She was making me mad. "She says the girls who tried out this year aren't very good. So she came to a freshman P.E. class to look for good material."

Janet gasped and turned around to relay the information to the girls behind her. I could hear them gasping like a catch of fish fresh taken from the water, and pretty soon they began to giggle and titter. It made me feel awful. I wished I hadn't told them after all.

"I think that's nice," said Mildred Schultz after a while. "I couldn't do it but you'll be real good on rally, Plum."

It was the longest speech I had ever heard her make. I was so surprised that for a minute I almost forgot about the girls who thought it was so funny.

7

"Thanks, Mildred." My ears were beginning to burn, and I couldn't stop them. "Of course I can't do it, though."

Mildred kept looking at me, thinking it over.

"Can you imagine!" That was Mary Beth's voice. It was as booming as a fog horn in the bay. I could hear her over everybody. "I wonder if Kelley has any idea who Plum is?"

Now some of the boys in back began wanting to know what all the excitement was about. You can just bet the girls told them, too. I scrooched as low as I could in the seat.

"Why?" asked Mildred. "Why can't you try out for rally?"

"I have to take the bus home. It's the only way I can get there," I told her shortly.

I guess Mildred saw the sense to that because in a minute she went back to her book.

I didn't have to go clear into Cooperville where most of the kids got off the bus. Our place is a mile out of town. Mildred Schultz got off first at her father's dairy farm, and mine would be the next stop. The Schultz farm was pretty good sized and as neat as a daisy. The barn is four times as big as the house, but they were both covered with fresh white paint every year. Our weather on the coast is hard on paint. There were brown jersey cows, a whole slew of them, in the fenced fields, and the grass was as green as some of the old trade beads that had belonged to Grandma Longor's mother. I could see white dots that must be Leghorn chickens pecking out by the barn. Mr.

Schultz was rich. At least he was richer than most people in Cooperville, except for his brother, George, of course.

Mildred began gathering up her armload of books before the bus reached her road. She carried so much homework every day that books and notebooks always slipped and fell off her lap. I was the one who had to pick them up. When Mildred tried, it always ended by her dropping everything, and Mrs. Heacock got mad when she had to wait. Usually it made me kind of mad, too, but today it didn't. Mildred had been the only one who hadn't laughed about my being on freshman rally.

"Good-bye, Mildred," I said when Mrs. Heacock brought the bus to a stop and Mildred had struggled to her feet.

Her blue popeyes looked sort of surprised. We usually didn't bother with such things as good-byes and hellos. She stared at me for a minute, then in a loud voice that carried to the back of the bus she said, "Good-bye, Plum. You ought to do what that girl said. You'd be good on freshman rally."

Everybody heard her, and everybody began to laugh. Above all the racket I could hear some of the things they were saying.

"Do you think Kelley Brennan really asked Plum to try out for freshman rally?" "No. More likely Kelley's mother's looking for somebody to do housework after school." "Can you imagine! Plum Longor on rally!" "She's lying. I don't know what Kelley wanted, but it wasn't that."

9

I stared hard at Mrs. Heacock's back and pretended not to hear. Oh, that Mildred Schultz! I could have murdered her. Be nice to somebody just once, and see what it gets you. I swore I'd never ride next to her again, not if I had to stand up all the way.

The kids were still laughing when Mrs. Heacock stopped in front of our place. After the Schultz's farm it looked worse than ever to me. There was no paint left on the frame house or the ramshackle old barn behind it. The porch was falling in on one side, and there was a heap of trash covered with gunny sacks by the door. Because Andy had thrown a ball through one of the windows, it was patched with cardboard until Mom could get somebody to cut a new pane of glass. There were no green fields around our house, only tall brown grass from last year, and mud, and the skeletons of evergreen blackberry vines.

Mrs. Heacock opened the door and I got out without looking behind me. I didn't need to. I could feel the eyes of the Cooperville kids staring at me and at my house. I could hear some of them still giggling about Plum Longor who pretended she was wanted on rally. Just before the door closed behind me, someone in the bus gave a war whoop.

It had started to rain again, and the path up to the front door was slippery with mud. Mom kept after us kids to carry rocks and make the path a little safer. Nobody did. In summer, when rocks were easy to find, it wasn't slippery. When it rained, which it did most of the year, nobody wanted to get wet.

I was so mad that I almost didn't make it up the

path without falling. This year, when I went to the community high school, I'd hoped things would be different. There were bound to be lots of kids who didn't know about Pop. There might even be some who didn't mind Indians, or part Indians. I had white blood, too, from Mom's father. But the Cooperville kids went to the new high school, too. They weren't going to let anyone forget. By tomorrow somebody would have told Kelley Brennan about me and what a fool she'd made of herself by calling me over in front of everyone.

I had to be careful of the steps because one of the boards was loose, but I knew which one so it didn't matter. By that time I was close enough to see the pile of trash by the front door. It hadn't been there when I left that morning. At least I couldn't remember it. It was covered with gunny sacks, all right, just as I'd seen from the bus, but it wasn't trash. It was Pop. He'd got drunk again and someone had brought him home and dumped him there.

The front door opened the minute I stepped on the porch. Grandma Longor must have been watching for me through the good window, the one that wasn't patched with cardboard.

"Help me get Willie inside," she said. "I can't lift him by myself. Not any more."

"How'd he get here? Didn't he go to work today?" Pop's snores sounded like an old bullfrog croaking. When I pulled off the gunny sack that covered him he didn't even stir.

"He went to work." Grandma bit off each word like it was a piece of thread. She didn't hold with whiskey, and always said it was the white man's curse put on the Indians. "I don't know where he got the firewater. A man in a truck brung him here. Dumped him just where he is. Didn't even knock on the door. Milo seen him driving away."

I put down my books and went around to the other side. Pop was a big man, but now that I was thirteen, Grandma and I could handle him. It was lucky that I was growing stronger because Grandma was getting weaker. I could remember when she could hoist Pop by herself, but not any more.

Even so we couldn't lift him clear off the porch floor. We each got a good grip under one of his arms which raised his head and shoulders. We just let his feet drag along behind. It didn't wake him up. He was too far gone for that.

We hauled him through the front room, where my half brother Milo slept on a cot, and into the downstairs bedroom next to it which belonged to Mom and Pop. It was a little room with just enough space for a double bed and a bureau. It took three of us to get Pop onto the bed, but my brother Chris was home from school and he helped. Chris is eleven, but he's small for his age, not much bigger than Andy, who is nine. We took off Pop's logger boots, which we should have done first because they made dirty spots on Mom's clean spread. Then we covered him with a blanket and shut the door. We could still hear him snoring through the boards, so we went into the kitchen and closed that door too.

"Did you put our noble sire to bed? And tend to all his wants?" asked Milo when we got there. Milo always talks funny like that. I guess it's because he's always got his nose in a book, any kind of book.

"He's in bed," said Chris. "But he didn't want anything."

Milo snorted through his nose and went back to reading. I sort of wished Pop had waited till tomorrow to get drunk, then Milo would have been at work. He could never seem to get used to Pop's failing, like the rest of us.

Milo only had a job two days a week, Tuesday and Saturday, and he was lucky to have that. He'd had polio when he was a baby, and it had left him so crippled that he couldn't use his legs. He had to walk on crutches, and one side of his face was a little twisted, too. He was smart, though. He'd gone all through high school with straight A's, and for a while he thought he'd get a scholarship to college. Something happened and he didn't get one, probably because he was an Indian. The only people who would give a crippled Indian a job were the ladies at the library in Seaside, and that was only part time. Tuesdays Milo mended books, and Saturdays, when they had a rush, he sat at the desk and stamped them out. He felt bad about not working more, and sometimes he took his feelings out on us.

"I wonder where Pop got the money to buy a bottle," said Chris. "Payday's not till tomorrow."

"Maybe it was a present," suggested Andy. "Maybe somebody gave it to him."

"It's more likely he borrowed the money from someone." Milo's nose came out of his book for a minute. "That is the most probable answer to your question."

Grandma's lips closed tightly together and she lifted a stove lid to peer at the fire inside. "More wood, Chris," she ordered.

Chris began whining that he'd got the wood last time. It was Andy's turn now. And Andy insisted that he'd filled the woodbox three times yesterday. Chris should do it all day to make up.

"If you two would realize how fortunate you are to have legs to carry you back and forth from the wood-pile, you'd be glad to do it," Milo told them an-grily. "Stop squawking. You make me sick."

"Wish Simon was here," said Grandma. "When Si-mon was here my woodbox was always full. Never had to tell him. Maybe he could handle Willie, too. Keep him from guzzling firewater up to his craw."

"Simon couldn't do any more about Pop than we can," Milo reminded her. "He never did when he was home."

"Willie was better then," Grandma insisted stub-bornly. "Every Saturday he used to stay sober so he could watch Simon play ball. Wouldn't want to miss that, Willie wouldn't. Had something to be proud of then. All the whites looking to his son to win their ball games for them."

Milo's face started turning red, and I wished Grandma wouldn't always talk about Simon. It wasn't Milo's fault that he couldn't be an athlete. If Chris didn't start growing pretty soon he wouldn't be one either, and about all an Indian has to make whites look up to him is how good he can play ball.

"When's Simon coming home, anyway?" asked

Andy curiously. "He's been gone a long time. Years and years."

"If he's smart, never," said Milo, picking up his book again.

"As soon as he gets out of the army hospital," I told Andy. "Soon as the doctors say he's well enough to leave."

"But it's been so long," persisted Andy. "Almost three years since they sent Simon back from the war. What's the matter with him anyway that it takes so long to cure him up?"

"Get the wood," ordered Grandma sternly. It always made her uncomfortable to talk about any kind of sickness. Besides, none of us could answer the question. Simon's letters always beat around the bush when it came to his injuries. We just knew he'd been hurt, and that they'd sent him to an army hospital to get well. It was too far away for us to visit, so we just had to wait.

Grandma whirled around and glared at me. "Plum, you go change out of your school dress. You want to wear it out before next year?"

I went upstairs to put on my jeans. Most of the girls wore pants to school, and Mom always wore a slack suit for working in the launderette. I had to wear a dress every day, except at home, because Grandma kicked up such a fuss about it.

There were two little bedrooms under the eaves. One belonged to Grandma and me, the other was for Chris and Andy. The way the roof sloped you could only stand up in the very middle of each room, but it was sure good sleeping up there when the rain pounded down so close above your head.

As I got out of my school clothes I wished again that Grandma wouldn't keep talking about Simon. We all knew he was her favorite, and in a way I didn't blame her. Simon was really something!

He was next to the oldest of all us Longor kids. He was twenty-four, no maybe twenty-five by now. Lucy was several years older. She was married to Hank Pierce and lived in Astoria. Then came Milo, who was twenty. They were Pop's children by his first wife, Sally Comely, who died when Milo was a baby. That's when Grandma Longor moved in with Pop. Someone had to take care of the three little kids.

Pop didn't get married again right away, not for several years. He was a logger, and I guess a good one, because even when he got drunk and missed a couple of days' work they always took him right back. Now it wasn't so easy to get back on the job. Sometimes they made him wait a while before they put him on the payroll again. I guess they figured it would teach him a lesson, but so far it hadn't. Grandma sold her old farm, which was in the Willamette Valley and had been part of the Grand Ronde Reservation before they closed the Reservation, and she bought this place where we live now. I guess she knew Pop pretty well because she had the lawyer make out the papers to her so the place couldn't be mortgaged away or sold.

Then Pop met my mother, who was Nancy Wing, and was just about the prettiest girl he ever saw. Pop is pretty good looking himself when he's sober. And talk! Pop could talk a chicken into putting its own head on the chopping block. He talked Mom into marrying him, and Grandma stayed on because Mom kept her job waiting tables in a restaurant. Then us kids started coming, first me, then Chris, then a baby girl who was born dead and finally Andy. Grandma was still needed because Mom always went back to work as soon as she had us. Besides, it's really Grandma's house, the deed being in her name and all. We just live here.

Every time Mom thinks about quitting work something happens, like taxes going up, or the car breaking down, or somebody getting sick, or Pop being laid off. Besides, Mom's got a real good job now managing a launderette. She says she'd rather work than stick around home. So would I. It's not much fun at home. But it's not much fun at school either.

When I got downstairs the woodbox was filled, and somebody had turned on the lights. That's another thing that cost a lot of money. We didn't have electric lights until Mom got her job managing the launderette. Andy and Chris were at it again, this time squabbling about what program they were going to watch on TV. They could have saved their breath because when they turned it on, the screen was blank and there was no sound. The set was secondhand when Mom bought it, and this was the third time something had gone wrong.

"Good," said Milo. "The trash you boys look at is not worth wasting your eyesight on."

"Not good, " said Grandma frowning. "I like to see

the pictures, too. Plum, you fix potatoes and carrots. Onions too."

I could smell the beef that had been simmering on the back of the cookstove, so I knew we were going to have stew for supper. Probably fried bread, too. Grandma was a great one for fried bread.

I had to go outside to get the vegetables. They were stored in a room off the kitchen porch where they would keep longer. It was dark by now, although it was only five o'clock. In winter, daylight didn't seem to last very long, especially when it rained. I could hear a car coming up the hill, but I knew it wasn't Mom. She couldn't turn the launderette over to the night woman until five, and then she'd have to drive home. I hoped she wouldn't have a flat tire.

I brought the vegetables inside and started getting them ready for a stew. Every once in a while I'd remember how the Cooperville kids had acted on the bus, and then I'd whack at a potato or a carrot, pretending it was Mary Beth or Wendy. I wished now that Kelley Brennan had never come to our P.E. class. No, I didn't wish that, because it made me feel good that someone like Kelley had noticed me. But I did wish I'd had sense enough to keep my mouth shut.

Milo was still reading and the little boys were putting together an old jigsaw puzzle so the kitchen was pretty quiet. All of a sudden there was a crash outside. Someone had fallen on the loose board in the front steps. Everyone stopped to listen. After a few minutes there was a pounding on the front door.

"I'll go," offered Chris.

"No," said Grandma. "Better I go."

We all watched as she opened the door between the kitchen and the front room and turned on the overhead light. Pop's bullfrog snores came faintly from behind the closed bedroom door.

"Who is it?" whispered Andy. I don't know why he thought he had to whisper, except that we don't have many visitors.

"Somebody who is lost and asking directions," said Milo, but he didn't go back to his reading. He waited like the rest of us to see who it was.

He was probably right, I thought. It had to be a stranger. Everyone who had been here before was smart enough to avoid that loose board in the step after they'd tripped on it once.

Grandma opened the outside door and her long skirt billowed in the wind. I could see that much when I peeked around from the table where I was working. I couldn't see anything else because it was dark, but I heard a man's voice. Then Grandma began to squeal like a pig that's being chased around a pen. I thought someone was attacking her so I grabbed the butcher knife and started to run to help.

I stopped when I saw that the stranger wasn't attacking Grandma. He was hugging her. And she was hugging him back. Andy and Chris were pushing against me, and even Milo had got up and was settling his crutches under his arms. Then Grandma turned around and we could see the stranger, who wasn't a stranger after all.

"It's Simon," screamed Grandma. "Look! It's Simon, home at last. Now everything will be good."

It felt funny to have Simon home after all those years. It wasn't like seeing a stranger, because he was our brother and even Andy, who had been just barely five when he left, remembered him. And it wasn't that he looked different, because he didn't. Sure he was thin and he looked kind of pale but that was because he'd been in a hospital for so long. People think Indians don't get suntans, but that's not true.

Simon made the rounds, hugging everybody. He couldn't miss Pop's snores and he went in the bedroom but he couldn't rouse him. So we all went in the kitchen again and shut the door.

Simon prowled around, looking at everything and

smiling to himself. Then he pulled out a kitchen chair, turned it around and straddled it so his chin could rest on the back. Somehow it made me feel good to see him sitting that way. Simon always did sit in chairs backwards, except when he was eating, of course. For the first time, I realized he was really home.

"It's sure good to be here," he said. "There were times when I didn't think I'd ever see you guys again."

"Why didn't you come home sooner?" asked Andy. He and Chris were sitting on the floor, one on each side of Simon, as close as they could get.

"They wouldn't let me out." Simon leaned over and scratched the top of Andy's head. I remembered that he used to do that to me when I was a little kid. "They had to make me a new glass eye first."

"You got a glass eye?" screamed Chris, and both he and Andy got up so they could stare in Simon's face.

We all stared, trying to figure out which eye was Simon's and which was the glass one. I couldn't tell. The doctors had done a good job of matching them up.

"Which one is it?" asked Chris.

"Can you see out of it? Can you take it out?" demanded Andy.

"No, I can't see out of it," said Simon laughing. "And I'm not going to take it out and let you use it for a marble, either."

"A new eye doesn't take almost three years in the hospital." Milo's voice sounded kind of funny. He was staring at Simon just as hard as the rest of us, but somehow I didn't think he was too interested in the new glass eye.

"Oh, they had to do some other patching up. In-

side, where it doesn't show," Simon told him care-
lessly. "I got a seam across my belly, Grandma, that
looks like somebody's worked a blanket design on me."

"You're skinny," she said frowning. "They starve
you maybe?"

"No. They fed us good. All we could eat. But
nothing like your fried bread. All the time I was
driving up from California, I kept thinking about
your fried bread."

"You've got a car?" I asked quickly. I hoped he'd
say yes. Having a brother who was a wounded war
hero was wonderful, but if he had his own car to
drive around in that was even better.

"What kind?" yelled Chris and Andy when Simon
nodded.

"A Chevy. Two years old, but in good shape. I
got a good deal on it. One of the guys who was in the
hospital with me for a while got it for me. His dad has
a car agency."

Two years wasn't that bad, I reminded myself. Of
course a Chevy wasn't a sporty foreign car like Perry
Schultz drove around, but Perry Schultz's father
owned the logging company and was the richest man
in Cooperville. At least a Chevy was better than Pop's
old pickup truck or Mom's Dodge that was ten years
old.

"It must have been some patch-up job to take that
long," said Milo thoughtfully. I don't think he'd even
heard what we'd been saying about Simon's car.

"Oh, you know." Simon shrugged his shoulders,
and I could see the bones under his plaid shirt. "What
the doctors call 'complications' set in. But I'm fine

now. Have to swallow a few pills and take it easy for a while. But if I hadn't been okay, they wouldn't have let me come home, would they?" He stared hard at Milo and after a minute Milo looked away.

"I suppose not," he said.

"So Pop's still at it." Simon changed the subject. "This happen often?"

"Sometimes." Grandma got up and started toward the cupboard. "I better start the batter for the fried bread now."

"Too often," said Milo. "The last time George Schultz laid him off for two weeks, with a warning."

"It will be different now you're home, Simon," Grandma insisted. "Remember how it used to be? Willie hardly ever looked at firewater then. He didn't want to miss none of your ball games."

"I don't play ball any more." Simon sounded kind of sad. Then he grinned at Chris. "But we got two other ballplayers coming on. How old are you, Chris? I lose track."

"Eleven." Chris hung his head. "I'm the littlest kid in our room at school."

"I'm big," boasted Andy. "I'm nine, and I'm almost as big as Chris."

"Chris, he takes after his ma's family," said Grandma. "The Lachances is all little people. Look at Nancy. Andy, he favors my father, the way you do, Simon. My father was a tall man."

"There are other things in the world besides athletics," Milo reminded them angrily. "Important things."

"Of course there are," Simon spoke up quickly. "And you got to remember that an athlete has only so many years of playing, Chris. Then he has to find another job. Maybe you'll be a doctor like the ones who patched me up."

"Maybe I will," agreed Chris eagerly. "Doctors don't have to be big, do they?"

"You shouldn't encourage him. Get his hopes up that way." Milo's voice sounded hard and scratchy. "Where's he going to get the money for that? A doctor's degree takes a lot of schooling. And don't talk about scholarships, either. I know all about that stuff. They led me up that road in high school, and where did it end? Mending library books two days a week."

"You do that, Milo?" Simon sounded surprised. I guess we'd forgotten to write him about Milo's job. "Why that's great. Just great. It's right up your alley, too. You always did like to read and you never could find enough books to keep you going. Now you've got all you want. Why, I bet you're so smart now, with all that reading, that nobody around can touch you."

Milo just kind of stared with his mouth open. Simon sounded like he was really proud, and people don't usually give Milo compliments. I don't know what he would have said because at that minute Mom came home.

"That Willie!" she shouted, banging open the kitchen door. "This is the last straw. This time I'm going to throw him out. I warned him the last time that if he ever did this again—"

"You can't throw him out," interrupted Grandma

quickly. "Willie's my boy and this is my house. Willie stays."

"Hello, Nancy." Simon stood up, and I was surprised all over again that he was so tall. His head was only about three inches below the ceiling. He was lots taller than Pop. Chinook Indians aren't usually tall people. I read somewhere that the Plains Indians are tall, but Coast Indians are generally short.

"Simon!" For a minute Mom forgot about Pop in the front bedroom. While Simon was hugging her, I saw Milo motion for Chris to close the kitchen door so we wouldn't hear the snores.

Mom is really awfully pretty, even if she is thirty-three years old. She has shiny black hair that she wears in straight bangs over her forehead, and her skin is as clear as mine. Clearer, really, because once in a while I get a pimple. She's little, and you'd never know she'd had four kids. She always wears pretty clothes, and even though they're bargains and don't cost much I think she looks as stylish as any movie star.

"This is a surprise," she told Simon, looking up at him. "We're so glad to see you."

"He's got a glass eye," said Andy. "But he won't tell us which one, so I don't believe it."

"This one," said Simon, laughing. He tapped his right eye gently with his finger and when he didn't blink we all believed him. To tell the truth, I really hadn't before. I thought he'd been kidding.

Mom was as amazed as everyone, but after a few minutes she began to frown and we knew she was thinking about Pop again.

26

"I see you haven't got around to putting in that shower yet, Nancy," said Simon before she had a chance to start in on her opinion of fathers and husbands who had no sense of responsibility. We'd all heard it before, and I guess Simon must have remembered it too.

"Not yet." She was a little apologetic because she'd been nagging at Pop for that shower before Simon went away to war. "Plumbers are so expensive, and besides I don't know where we'd put it."

"I've been thinking about that," said Simon. "I had a lot of time to think in the hospital. I believe we could extend the bathroom closet out into the room a ways. It will make the kitchen smaller, but it would be cheaper than knocking out an outside wall and building onto the house. The coils in the cookstove will heat the water, so we won't have to pay for a lot of extra pipe."

Mom's eyes got bright just thinking of it. Then she shook her head.

"It would cost too much, Simon. My salary will only go so far and with Willie being laid off again—"

"It couldn't have happened at a better time," Simon assured her cheerfully. "Pop's a good carpenter. If he's laid off, he can add onto the bathroom while he's not working."

"But we can't afford—"

"I've got a little money saved. There was no place to spend my back pay in the hospital," he reminded her. "I'll pay for the lumber and the plumber. It's my homecoming present to the family."

27

"Huh," said Grandma, stirring her bread batter fiercely. "We got along without such stuff before. I can think of a lot better ways to spend money."

"Oh, Simon!" I knew Mom wouldn't make any more fuss about Pop now. She was too glad to have the shower. "But I can't let you do this," she added.

"You can't stop me," he reminded her. "And we'll try to get it rushed through this week. I'd like to have it done before the party."

"What party?" Chris was the one who asked, but we were all wondering the same thing.

"Why, the 'Welcome Home, Simon' party that we're going to have next weekend," he told us promptly. "It's going to be a big powwow. I want to see every Indian in this part of the country at it. I've been planning this party for the last six months."

Pop was so sick the next morning that he could hardly get excited about Simon being home.

"If I'd only known you was coming," he moaned, "I wouldn't have touched that stuff. I wouldn't have even smelled the cork."

"It's okay, Pop," Simon told him. "We'll talk about it when you feel better. But you've got to pull yourself together long enough to tell me what to buy at the lumberyard. I don't know anything about building onto a room. And that's what you'll be doing while you're laid off."

"It's permanent this time. They'll never take me back," insisted Pop. "George Schultz warned me. I got

29

no job now. Once I was the best bucker in the woods, but look at me today. Look what I done to my family."

But he measured the walls, even though Simon had to read off the numbers on the yardstick for him. Then he moaned and groaned some more and after he told us how much lumber it would take and what size nails, he went back to bed.

Since it was Saturday, Milo had driven in with Mom to work in the library. Grandma was grumpy about building onto the bathroom and would hardly talk to anybody. Andy and Chris wanted to drive to the lumberyard with Simon, and when he asked if I wanted to go too, I said yes. I was almost sorry when I saw he was taking Pop's pickup, not the almost new Chevy, but I didn't want to stay home with Grandma. The little boys climbed in back, and I sat up in front with Simon.

We had to go clear into Seaside, because there's no lumberyard in Cooperville, only a little office for the Schultz Lumber Company. They don't process the logs here. They just fell the trees and haul them out of the woods by truck.

It had stopped raining during the night, but the smell of it was still in the air. It was cold, too, probably snowing a few miles higher up in the mountains. Grandma had found an old mackinaw of Pop's for Simon to wear, and a knitted wool cap. There weren't any of his own clothes left for him to put on. They'd all been cut down for the younger boys.

"I'm glad you're coming, Plum," said Simon, after he had finally teased the pickup into starting and got it out on the road. "We've got a lot of catching up to do. How's school?"

"All right." I wished he wouldn't ask me about school. I'd almost forgotten about yesterday on the bus, but now it all came back.

"You go to Sunset Community?"

"It's my first year. I'm a freshman."

"Great school," Simon assured me. "Four of my happiest years were spent at old Sunset. I made a lot of friends there. Good friends."

I decided that the best way to keep him from talking about me was to talk about him.

"You know Perry Schultz, don't you? Wasn't he in your class?"

"Sure was. Great guy. You'd never think to meet him that his dad had all that dough. Whatever happened to Perry? He go in the service?"

"I don't know. He went away to college. Someplace in the east. But now he's home. He's supposed to be working for his father, but most of the time you see him driving around in a bright red foreign car."

I knew I was babbling, but I couldn't stop. I had to make Simon think of other things so he wouldn't pry into my affairs. Somehow I didn't want Simon, who had been so popular in school, to find out what a flop his sister was.

"Red foreign car, huh?" asked Simon, and he put on the brakes so suddenly that I could hear the little boys squeal with delight in back. Kids are funny. They like to be bumped. "Like that one over there maybe?"

We were passing the Schultz's dairy farm. Simon had stopped just before the private road that led up to the white house resting in its tidy green fields. In the driveway, parked before the front door, was a bright red automobile.

"That's right. That's Perry Schultz's car. He must have stopped to see his uncle." I was glad I had come up with that subject, because it had certainly turned Simon off from Sunset High School. The next moment I wasn't so sure it had been the right thing to do because he was turning the pickup into the Schultz's road.

"Oh, Simon. I don't think we should. People say Perry Schultz has changed," I protested. "They say he's stuck-up since he got back. You never see him with anybody. He just drives around by himself."

"Ha," said Simon skeptically. "Probably lonesome, poor guy."

I got the most terrible feeling in my stomach, like I needed to throw up. Simon didn't know the changes that had taken place since he went away. He wasn't a hero any more, not to anyone but his own family. He'd knock on the door and ask for the man who used to be his friend, and Perry Schultz would snub him, the way the Cooperville kids treated me. But I couldn't stop it. I just had to sit there and let it happen.

Before we quite made it to the car, the front door of the house opened and two people came outside. One was Perry Schultz, all dressed up fit to kill in a leather jacket with a thin wool scarf around his neck. The other was Mildred.

They came down the steps and stood watching while Simon jammed on the brakes and the engine sputtered and died. Simon didn't seem to notice. He opened the door, jumped out and started toward the two people on the bottom step.

"Hi, you old son of a gun," he yelled. Then he snatched off the wool cap which came down over his eyebrows and waved it in the air.

For a minute the two of them stared, then Perry Schultz let out a yell that you could have heard a mile.

"Siwash!" His voice sounded glad and excited, but I still felt my spine stiffen at the word he had called my brother. "Siwash" is what people call Indians when they don't like them, and they might as well add "Dirty Old" in front of it. That's what they mean when they say it.

"Dutch!" shouted Simon. "Dutch Schultz!"

For a minute I wanted to sink into the plastic upholstery. Imagine calling wealthy, snobbish Perry Schultz "Dutch." But the funny thing was he didn't seem to hear. The two of them began hugging each other and hammering each other's backs. When I saw that I decided it was all right.

By now Mr. Carl Schultz, Mildred's father and Perry's uncle, had heard the commotion and come outside. He shook Simon's hand and I could see that Simon was being introduced to Mildred. I wondered what he would think of her after knowing Perry as well as he did. Slow-thinking, fat Mildred must come as a terrible shock. Pretty soon they all started walking toward the pickup, and I hurried to pull a little

33

hair out from under my cap. I didn't want Perry
Schultz to think Simon's sister looked like a peeled
onion.

Simon introduced us to Mr. Schultz and Perry and
they were both very nice. Mr. Schultz was short with
wide shoulders and a square head. His pale blue eyes
were sort of popped out, like Mildred's, and he
had just a trace of an accent. I'd heard he had been
born in this country and I decided he must have picked
it up from his parents who came from Germany just
before one of the wars over there. Perry was even
handsomer up close than from a distance, and his
clothes—wow!

Mildred and I nodded to each other, but we didn't
say anything. We didn't have to. Everybody else was
talking enough to make up for it. But pretty soon there
came that sort of gap in the conversation where everyone waits for everyone else. Mildred filled that gap.

"She's the one, Papa," she said. "The one I told you
about. Plum's my best friend at school."

I could feel my mouth wanting to drop open, but I
held it shut. I even managed to smile.

"Good, good." Mr. Schultz beamed at me. "Yes,
Mildred has told us about you. About how you always
ride together on the bus."

"You used to be my best friend in school, too, Si,"
said Perry. "Remember the day we—"

I didn't listen to what happened that day. I was
thinking about Mildred telling her family I was her
best friend. She didn't have a best friend. She didn't
have any friend. I didn't know whether to be sorry
for her or mad.

"I have to go to the dentist. My cousin is driving me into Seaside," said Mildred. "Where are you going, Plum?"

"To the lumberyard in Seaside. And we have to hurry because it closes at noon on Saturdays, Simon." Even though I raised my voice he didn't hear me, and with Mildred and Mr. Schultz both staring at me I felt I ought to keep on talking. "We're making our bathroom bigger and if we don't get the lumber today Pop can't work on it tomorrow. And Simon wants to get it finished before the party we're going to have next Saturday."

"You are having a party?" asked Mildred. For once it didn't take a full minute for my words to register. She spoke right up.

"Not exactly. It's Simon's party, but it will be at our house."

"I have never been invited to a party," said Mildred wistfully, and I couldn't help feeling sorry. But neither had I.

"It's not that kind of a party," I explained. "Not the kind that Wendy and Mary Beth and the other kids in Cooperville have. It's just family friends. Indian friends we know along the coast who will want to see Simon. I guess you could call it a powwow really, not a party."

"You have too been to parties, Mildred," said her father chidingly. "To your Uncle George's for dinner. To church suppers. Those are parties."

Mildred thought about this a minute before she answered.

"Those were parties with my family," she said fi-

35

nally. "I have never been invited to a party by myself. Not once has anybody asked me."

"Would you like to come to my welcome home party, Mildred?" asked Simon. He had finished horsing around with Perry in time to hear what she said. Simon has always been a sucker for anything that's hurt. "I'd better warn you first that you'd be the only white. The other guests are all Indians. But Plum will be there. She can introduce you around."

"Yes." Mildred didn't give him a chance to change his mind. "I may go, Papa?"

"You may go," he told her tolerantly. "It is all right. You will be with your friend."

I don't know what was said after that. I just sat there feeling sort of numb. I didn't want Mildred to come to Simon's party. I had dragged in the word "powwow" purposely to discourage her. We don't say that around here. We've been off the reservation too long. But it hadn't made a dent. She was coming. And there would be kids there I could talk to, kids I hadn't seen for a long time, Sherry Pierce, from Astoria, and Nina Wachino, from around Wheeler. Now I'd be stuck with fat Mildred, who had actually invited herself. It wasn't fair.

Eventually Simon tore himself away, after Andy and Chris reminded him again about the lumberyard closing early on Saturday, and we left. Perry's red car buzzed past us before we'd gone a hundred yards on the road and fat Mildred turned around and waved.

"What's the matter, Plum?" asked Simon finally. "You've gotten awfully quiet."

"Why did you ask that girl? I can't stand her. Nobody can. And she's not my best friend."

"But I heard her say you always sat together on the bus."

"Because nobody else will sit with her. Or with me, either. Nobody likes Mildred because she's fat and stupid. And they don't like me because I'm Indian and my father's a drunk." I hadn't meant to say that last part, but it came out before I could stop it.

"I see," said Simon. After a while he changed the subject.

The next day Pop started tearing out part of the kitchen wall to make the bathroom bigger. He was a good carpenter, and it went pretty fast. Simon, Grandma, Mom and Milo sat at the kitchen table and made out a list of people to invite to the welcome-home party.

There weren't too many Indians left on the coast to invite unless we went into the Siletz. For some reason, Simon didn't want to do that. He said he only wanted people whose fathers or grandfathers had been on the Grand Ronde Reservation.

"That's silly," Milo told him. "Grand Ronde and Siletz were both part of the Coast Reservation in the beginning, only Siletz was in the south and Grand Ronde in the north. There's a lot of land to cover. There wasn't any difference in tribes, and some, like the Rogue Rivers, were actually split up between the two reservations. We've got some good friends on the Siletz, people you'd like to see."

"Maybe another time. Today we'll stick to people

who lived on the Grand Ronde before it was dissolved." I remembered that Simon could be pretty stubborn when he wanted to. This was one of those times.

"That was long time ago," said Grandma, nodding. "The young men kept moving away, and their brides with them. They went to the white towns to find work. More and more went. Soon there was only old people and children left on the reservation."

"And the kids got out, too, soon as we could," said Pop, taking out a mouthful of nails so he could speak. "Who wants to be a reservation Indian, a Siwash? Live like the whites, that's the way to do it. Me and Sally come down here. Got me a good job in the woods straight off, too. Used to be a lot of us here then. Most of them fished, but not me. I'm a logger and a good one. No need for a reservation after we left. Good thing they dissolved it. Government gave us a little money for the land, not much but a little."

"Now the people have scattered again," reported Milo. "A lot are working in Portland. Most of them have gone all white. You know, married whites, and their children married whites. Not much Indian blood left."

"Who is left besides Hank Pierce?" persisted Simon.

"The Wachinos and the Shaws and the Deans," Milo checked them off on his fingers. "That's about all."

"Dave Beckett," said Grandma, and we all looked at her like she had lost her mind.

"Grandma," I protested. "He smells. He's a dirty old man."

"He lived on the Grand Ronde." Grandma could be just as stubborn as Simon. "He'd like to come to a party."

"We'll invite him," promised Simon. He seemed pleased to have smelly old Dave Beckett included. "Nancy, what about your grandparents? They still alive?"

"I think so. I didn't get up there last summer. We were so busy and all." Mom looked apologetic. If we saw her grandparents once a year we did well, but I don't think they cared.

Great-Grandma and Grandpa Lachance lived in a little shack way up the Nehalem. There weren't any roads and you had to walk two or three miles to get to their house. It didn't smell too good, either, but it wasn't as bad as Dave Beckett's. They lived off the land. Great-Grandpa Lachance fished and shot deer, whether it was hunting season or not, and because they were so far away the game warden didn't pay any attention. Grandpa only killed what he needed, and how much can two old people eat? Great-Grandma had a little garden and she dried wild berries and gathered roots and stuff, just like her people had always done.

"We'll invite them," said Simon.

"They won't come," Mom warned him. "I've asked them here before. They don't want to leave their place. They'll die there. Every time I go to see them I have a terrible feeling, wondering what I'll find."

"They'll come," said Simon positively. "I'll go get them myself."

It's going to be some party, I thought. Dave Beckett and Great-Grandma and Grandpa Lachance! Mildred Schultz might as well come. It was going to be a terrible flop anyway.

Simon spent all week getting ready for his party, which he now insisted on calling a powwow. It was kind of silly for him to use the word because, as Pop kept pointing out, we gave up powwows when we left the reservation to live like whites. We didn't even go to the big powwows held by the Warm Springs and some of the other tribes across the mountains. Whenever I heard about them, though, I thought it was too bad that we didn't go. They sounded like fun.

Simon had talked to Perry, who talked to his father, and George Schultz agreed to give Pop one more chance. But it would be the very last time. If he ever got drunk on the job again, he was through. Pop promised faithfully that he'd never touch another drop, and maybe he meant it because he didn't even kick up a fuss when Simon said there wouldn't be anything to drink at the powwow but coke and coffee.

When they counted up, there were fourteen grown-ups invited and eighteen kids, too many to crowd in the house, so Simon said we'd have the powwow in the barn.

"But the barn is falling apart," Mom reminded him. "It's cold, and the roof leaks."

"We'll put buckets under the leaks and build a big fire," said Simon. "There's a dirt floor, so it can't hurt anything, and the cracks will take care of the smoke."

Then he asked Milo to come out with him to look at the barn, and the little boys and I tagged along.

"I don't know what you've got up your sleeve," said Milo suspiciously as we sloshed through the backyard mud, "but it's something. I remember how you used to operate."

Simon just grinned and didn't answer.

Barns are always bigger than houses in Oregon. I guess ours had once had stalls for horses or cows, but Pop had chopped them out for firewood. Now it was one big room, with cold wind leaking through the cracks and places where boards were loose, and three or four holes in the roof where the rain came through. It was pretty bad, and I wasn't surprised that Milo kept saying we couldn't ask anyone to come out here.

"Sure we can. Pop can nail up the loose boards, maybe even mend the roof a little," said Simon absently. "What's this over here in the corner, Milo?"

42

"Oh, I was just fiddling around last summer." I could tell by his voice how embarrassed Milo was. "I was trying to see if I could make a canoe. Remember how I used to carve little things? This time I wanted to try my hand at something bigger."

"It's a dugout!" exclaimed Simon when he had inspected Milo's canoe. "Just one log—cedar, isn't it?—and you've hollowed it out and even carved it."

"It's nothing," said Milo. "I was just passing the time."

"But it's great! It's like the old Indian canoes they used to make. How'd you learn how to do it?"

The little boys and I went over to look, too, but I couldn't see that it was so much. It was just a hollowed-out log that Milo had shaped at each end. There were charred places that looked as though he had tried to burn it a little. He'd made a couple of paddles, too, and they lay in the bottom. The dinghies that Hank Pierce carries on his fishing boat were a lot better.

"I read about it in books from the library." Milo's face was beginning to glow under Simon's praise, and even the twisted side of his mouth was turning up a little. "It's just a small one. A one-man canoe. The old timers used to make big ones. They held as many as thirty people, and they went up and down the rivers and even out to sea."

"Milo, will you start reading everything you can find about our people? About the Coast Indians? Take some notes so you can tell us about them at the pow-wow." I'd never seen Simon more serious.

"I guess I could," agreed Milo after a minute. "But I don't think anybody would want to listen."

43

I didn't think so either, but I didn't like to say so.

"Just do it," urged Simon. "Do it for me."

Pop finished the bathroom walls early that week, and while the plumber was installing the shower, he fixed the front steps and managed to patch up the barn a little. There wasn't too much he could do there except to nail back the loose boards and stuff more gunny sacks in the biggest cracks. He couldn't do anything to the roof because we didn't have any shingles, and the holes were too big to cover with smashed out tin cans. He did knock together a couple of rough benches for the old people to sit on, and after school the little boys and I swept the dirt floor and dragged the old, moldy hay outside to burn. It made too much smoke to use for the powwow bonfire.

In the meantime, I had school to think about and that was more important than Simon's powwow. Getting on that school bus on Monday morning was the hardest thing I ever had to do, but I needn't have worried. The girls were too busy talking about Mary Beth's slumber party they had gone to last Saturday and the school carnival dance that was scheduled for the next weekend. They were so wrapped up in deciding what they were going to wear to that, they forgot all about me. I took the last vacant seat, right behind Mrs. Heacock as I always did, and when we stopped at the Schultz's, Mildred sat next to me and there wasn't anything I could do about it. We didn't speak when she got on, but halfway to school she made one remark.

"I can hardly wait for Saturday. What are you going to have for refreshments at your party?"

"Hot dogs," I whispered, hoping no one would hear, and no one did.

The hot dogs had been Mom's idea.

"It's about the cheapest way you can feed thirty-two people, Simon," she had said. "And we might as well use that bonfire for something else besides keeping warm. I could bake some beans if you like. What with all the coke you'll have to buy it's going to be an expensive party."

"Powwow," he reminded her, smiling.

"*Wa wa*," corrected Milo, who must have taken Simon seriously about reading up on the local Indians. "I can't find the word 'powwow' used by the Chinooks. They had *wa wa*s for talking together, and their parties were always potlatches."

"Didn't the old timers give presents at potlatches?" asked Simon.

"Sure," agreed Milo. "They gave away all they owned. But there was food, too. Lots of it. It was a celebration."

"We'll call ours a potlatch." Simon made up his mind quickly. "We can't afford to give presents, but that's all right. Good work, Milo. Keep it up." He was smiling to himself as he went off to take one of those pills he had to swallow every few hours.

On Thursday he drove away in his new Chevy to invite Great-Grandpa and Grandma Lachance. Mom kept insisting they wouldn't come, but Simon was sure they would. I didn't care, which is a terrible way to feel about your great-grandparents, but I hardly knew them. The times Mom had dragged us kids up the Nehalem to their place, they hadn't acted particularly

45

glad to see us. I suppose part of it was because Mom's mother, their daughter, had married a white man. Even when he left her after a year, they hadn't really forgiven my grandmother. I thought it was very mean of them since Great-Grandpa Lachance's grandfather had been white. He was a Frenchman, who worked for Dr. McLoughlin at Fort Vancouver, but I suppose they thought that was different because when he married he left his own people and lived with the Indians.

"We're not going to have enough food," worried Mom after Simon was gone. "People eat a lot. I'd better make a big salad."

"Indians didn't eat salads," objected Milo, and I could tell he was getting into the swing of Simon's idea. "Maybe a basket of raw vegetables to pass around. But roots and nuts would be better."

"I don't suppose they ate hot dogs, either," said Mom snappishly.

"I will make fried bread," said Grandma. "Everybody likes my fried bread."

Friday was a strange day at school. Everybody was excited about the carnival dance that night. The study hall was almost empty because kids got excused to help decorate the gym. I'd done my homework, and of course Mildred Schultz had too, but we were probably the only ones. The teachers pretended to be upset when no one knew the answers to questions, but I don't think they really were. I think they expected it. Sunset's annual carnival is a big affair. It's only held once a year, and from what everybody says it's really special. I almost wished I were going, but when I remembered that I'd be all alone with everybody around me having fun, I was glad I wasn't.

I passed Kelley Brennan in the hall between classes, and when she smiled and said "hi" to me I almost dropped my notebook. I hadn't seen her since she'd asked me to stay after P.E., and I didn't think she'd remember me. But I was just as glad there was nobody around who knew me. I didn't want to start that thing all over again.

When I got off the bus that afternoon I saw Simon's Chevy in the front yard so I knew he was back from seeing Great-Grandma and Grandpa Lachance. I wondered if he'd talked them into coming to his party. There was a bundle wrapped in gunny sacking on the front porch. It was so big that for a minute I thought Pop had forgotten his promise and got drunk again. Then I saw it was all tied up with rope, so I knew it wasn't Pop. It was probably something Simon had picked up for his party.

Great-Grandma and Grandpa had come all right. They were sitting on two straight-backed kitchen chairs, looking uncomfortable and as though they wished they were somewhere else. Grandma Longor sat in the rocking chair. She hated the rocker because she said it made her feel dizzy, and I knew she was only sitting there because it was her house and she didn't want the Lachances to forget it. It was like the rocking chair was a throne, and as queen, it was proper that she occupy it.

I was so surprised to see them that I could hardly

say hello. I just stood there, while my great-grandparents stared at me. They didn't smile, and neither did I.

I guess they were both awfully old. They would have to be or they couldn't have been Mom's grandparents, but they didn't look much older than Grandma Longor.

Great-Grandma Lachance was fat, and so short that when she sat on the kitchen chair her moccasins barely touched the floor. They were real Indian moccasins, and I knew she'd made them herself after tanning the skin that Great-Grandpa had brought home. Because of the fat, her face wasn't very wrinkled, but the skin looked old and dry like it had been smoked over a fire. She had little tiny black eyes shining out from the folds of fat, and her hair was gray and braided into skimpy plaits down her back. She wore some kind of loose cotton dress that hung straight from the neck, and there were strings of beads around her neck. Oh, she was a real Indian all right, the kind you read about but never see. I hoped nobody from Cooperville would catch sight of her while she was here.

Although Great-Grandpa Lachance was one-quarter white, it didn't show. His skin was as brown as an oak leaf in autumn and as wrinkled as a raisin. He was as skinny as Great-Grandma was fat, and he wore a leather jacket with fringe on it and some greasy pants to match. I'd never seen him dress any other way except in hot weather. Then he left off the top and went around in just the pants. Great-Grandma made him a new outfit every year, but she said it took more than one pair of moccasins to last the twelve months.

"You remember Plum," said Simon.

"She look like Frances." Great-Grandma Lachance still didn't smile. She looked cross. I remembered that Frances was her daughter, Mom's mother, who had run away with the white man and had never been forgiven.

"Frances look better," objected Great-Grandpa Lachance. It made me mad that they were talking about me as though I weren't there. "This girl too skinny. Feed her more *mowitch*."

"She eats good," said Grandma Longor defensively. "Plum's just growing too fast, is all. She'll plumpen up when she stops growing."

I hadn't grown for a year and she knew it, but she didn't want the Lachances to think she was starving me.

"Isn't it nice your great-grandparents could come to the potlatch?" asked Simon. His question seemed to be directed at me. "They haven't been to one for years. And you should see what they brought us. A whole deer! We're going to cook it tomorrow along with the hot dogs."

So that's what was wrapped in a gunny sack on the porch. A deer!

"But what if the game warden should come by?" I had visions of us all being carted off to jail for having a deer out of season. There are only so many weeks out of the year when people are allowed to shoot deer, and the season had been over for two months.

"What if he does?" Simon laughed. "Lots of people have tagged venison in their frozen food lockers. It all looks the same when it's thawed. We can say we lost the tag."

"This *mowitch* fresh killed." Great-Grandpa frowned. "Killed yesterday same day Simon come to my house."

"You want to learn make baskets?" Great-Grandma Lachance was tired of talking about out-of-season deer meat. "Good baskets like Tutunti women make?"

"Of course she does," answered Simon before I could open my mouth. "It's what she's always wanted to do, only there was nobody to teach her."

"*Aya*." Great-Grandma Lachance looked scornfully at Grandma Longor, who pretended she didn't notice. Grandma Longor was a Chinook, and after the white man came with his pots and pans to trade, the Chinooks stopped making baskets. But Great-Grandma Lachance was a Tutunti, a Rogue River, and they never stopped making them.

"We brought willow switches so she could teach you, Plum," Simon said, giving me a look that said I'd better go along with the idea or he'd skin me alive. "They're soaking over there."

"Maybe ready now." Great-Grandma lowered herself to the floor and waddled to the sink where a whole bunch of sticks were floating in Grandma Longor's dishpan.

"You change out of your school clothes first, Plum," ordered Grandma Longor sharply. "Then maybe after you've peeled the vegetables for the fish soup and helped me get things started, you can play at basket-making with your great-grandma."

I took as long as I dared to change my clothes. Who wanted to make baskets? If Simon thought it was so great he could just make them himself. But when I got downstairs, Great-Grandma Lachance had decided the willow needed to soak a little more so I was saved until after supper.

Nobody paid much attention to me. Simon was pumping Great-Grandpa about the things he used to do when he was young, and the little boys were listening, too, their eyes almost bugging from their heads. Grandma Longor was acutally rocking in her chair, so I knew she was upset, and Great-Grandma was working away at a piece of leather, kneading it with her fingers and sometimes actually chewing on it a little to get it soft.

I got the vegetables ready for the soup and about then Mom and Milo got home. Since she was in charge, it was no trouble for Mom to shift her day off at the launderette, but Milo had been a little jittery about asking to have his work day changed to Friday so he could come to the potlatch. He needn't have been. He said the librarians were great and made him promise to tell them all about it when he went back.

The first thing Mom wanted to know was about the gunny sack bundle on the front porch, and she was as scared as I was when she found it held fresh venison.

"You know it's out of season, Simon," she said. "You shouldn't have let them bring it. We could all be arrested and fined."

"It's a present. You can't refuse to accept it or you'll insult your grandparents," he insisted. "Besides, it will all be cooked and eaten by this time tomorrow and it sounds a lot better to me than hot dogs."

After supper, Great-Grandma Lachance started me on basketmaking. We both sat on the floor, although I wondered how we'd ever get her up again. Mom said she wanted to learn too, and for the first time Great-Grandma actually smiled.

Once we got started it was really fun, weaving the willow sprouts and lacing them into a design. Great-Grandma had gathered them early in the year and let them dry. Then by soaking, she could limber them up again so she could make them do what she wanted. She had brought a couple of finished baskets as samples, but I knew I could never make anything so fancy as those.

Mom didn't get along too well, but I did. If you took it slow and were careful not to force the wet willow but work it gently into place, it didn't break. I could tell Great-Grandma was pleased that I caught on so fast, although she didn't say so.

"Some day I show you how to dye willow with black clay," she told me. "Then you can make stripe in your basket."

The little boys wanted to make baskets, too, but both great-grandparents were horrified.

"Warriors never make baskets," said Great-Grandpa severely. "Come. I show you what men and boys do." He jangled the pocket of his leather jacket, and the sound was that of rocks clanking together.

"Arrowheads!" cried Milo. "Do you still make arrowheads, Grandfather?"

"I cannot stop," he admitted, grinning sheepishly. "I made them when I was a boy and a young man. I make them still. It is something to do with my hands. The old woman makes baskets. I make points for arrows."

"But you don't use them for hunting?" asked Milo. "You use a gun."

"That is so." Great-Grandpa sighed loudly. "I do not bend a bow. I only make points for arrows."

I had looked up in time to see Simon and Milo exchange a funny look, but Great-Grandma spoke sharply, telling me one of my willow sprouts was out of line, so I forgot it.

All evening we sat there, Great-Grandma, Mom and me working with softened willow while the males in the family chopped away on pieces of stone. Grandma Longor rocked in her rocking chair so fast that I was sure it would give her a headache.

"What do you do with all the baskets you make, Grandma?" I asked, when I had finally made the turn at the bottom to suit her and was starting up the side.

"Do nothing. Once, when I was young woman and lived on reservation, I sold them to whites. In summer we went to towns where whites lived. Me and my mother walked from house to house selling our baskets."

"Peddlers," muttered Grandma Longor under her breath, and I hoped I was the only one who heard.

"Don't go to white town now," continued Great-Grandma Lachance a little sadly. "The old man he

53

walk in maybe one time a year for salt and tobacco. Maybe little coffee. Nobody left to buy my baskets."

"How much would they bring?" asked Simon. I didn't know he'd been listening. "The one the size Plum is working on? How much?"

"Two bits," Great-Grandma told him promptly. "Big one stand so high," she held her hand about three feet from the floor, "two dollar maybe. Big ones take longer to make. Maybe two days."

"And you've got a lot of them all finished?"

"Shed all full," reported Great-Grandma, shaking her head.

"Suppose I buy them all from you and sell them to the whites?" Simon's eyes were gleaming. "But your prices are too low for today's market. It's like Grandpa Lachance's arrowheads. I offered him more, but he says 25¢ apiece is plenty."

Great-Grandma nodded positively.

"Two bits for little basket," she repeated. "Two dollar, maybe dollar, four bits for big. That is all. It will be good to have shed empty again."

My stomach gathered into a hard knot inside of me. Was this what Simon was planning to do now he was home? Go from door to door selling baskets and arrowheads like some old blanket Indian? Of course, he'd told us the doctor said he couldn't do hard work for a while, and he had to keep taking those pills every few hours, but there must be something respectable he could do. Perry Schultz would help him find a job. I could just hear the Cooperville kids laughing about Simon peddling baskets and I felt like crying.

We were planning to eat about one o'clock, so people probably wouldn't come till the middle of the morning, but Mom was up before six on Saturday. She'd soaked her beans the day before and boiled them, so all she had to do was mix them up with molasses and onions and a hunk of salt pork and put them in the oven. Then she got Pop to cut off a big haunch of the venison on the front porch and she slit the top with a knife so she could stick garlic into it before she baked it. Great-Grandma didn't say anything, but you could tell she thought Mom was nuts, and Simon really blew his cool. It seems he'd been expecting to cut off strips and cook them over the bonfire on

55

sticks, like we did our hot dogs. When he saw there was still plenty of meat left after Mom had got her roast, he calmed down.

Great-Grandma wanted me to go back to my basket weaving the minute we'd finished breakfast, but Grandma Longor was too quick for her. She said I had chores to do first. She must have laid awake thinking of them there were so many. After I washed the dishes I had to get the vegetables ready for Mom's tossed salad and cut the buns for the hot dogs and measure out the coffee that would be boiled in the big kettle and sweep the floor and clean up the kitchen again.

Mom kept busy too, but so far as I could see nobody else had much to do but wait for the company. Great-Grandma worked on her leather and Grandma Longor rocked in her chair. Every once in awhile they'd peek at each other, then look away quick without saying anything.

About eleven o'clock the first guest arrived, and wouldn't you know it would be Dave Beckett? He didn't have a car, so he'd either walked or thumbed a ride, but anybody who picked him up would have had to open all the car windows. I could smell him the minute Chris opened the front door, and for the first time I was glad we were having the party in the barn where there was plenty of ventilation.

My great-grandparents greeted him politely, but you could tell they really didn't care whether he was there or not. Not Grandma Longor. She was so glad to see him she invited him to sit in her rocking chair. At first I couldn't understand it. Then I realized it was because she and Dave Beckett were both Chinooks. Since the Lachances were Tutunti Rogue Rivers, I guess she had felt outnumbered before. Although they'd been put on the same reservation, the horse Indians and the canoe Indians never did get along.

Dave Beckett had brought a present to the potlatch, a bucket of mussels with a few bay crabs lying on top. He gave it to Simon before he sat down in Grandma's rocking chair, and Simon thanked him over and over. He was just being polite, of course. Nobody eats mussels, and while we do eat bay crabs they don't compare with our Dungeness. Bay crabs are soft and sort of bland, but at least they aren't stringy like those big Alaska crabs the fish vendors import and palm off on the tourists during the season.

"Are the crabs cooked?" asked Mom, trying to be pleasant and not wrinkle up her nose at the way the kitchen was beginning to smell. "If they aren't, why don't you light the bonfire in the barn early and set on a kettle of water out there, Simon? The stove is full."

"Course they're cooked," said Grandma Longor sharply. "Any fool can tell that by the color."

"Boiled 'em last night," said Dave Beckett. "Et one for my supper. Boiled 'em all to once. Was that *mowitch* I seen out in front?"

"*Mowitch*," Great-Grandpa told him proudly. "Shot it myself."

"Maybe you ought to begin carrying things to the barn." Mom tried again to clear her kitchen. "The

57

trestle table's set up, and someone should start slicing that raw venison into strips."

"I do that," Great-Grandma Lachance said positively. "Nobody cuts *mowitch* better'n me."

"Go change your clothes, Plum," ordered Grandma Longor. "You don't want people to catch you in your work duds."

When I got back downstairs everybody had gone to the barn but Mom, and the first car was driving into our yard.

Everybody but us has a pretty nice car. They are nothing like Perry Schultz's, of course, but they aren't anything to be ashamed of either. Indians down here make as much money as whites because they do the same kind of work and belong to a union. Pop makes good money, too, when he works, but he's been off more than he's been on because of his problem.

This car belonged to the Pierces from Astoria. Lucy Pierce is Simon and Milo's sister, my half sister, and she's married to Hank Pierce who is a fisherman. They've got three kids and Sherry is only a year younger than I am so I'd been looking forward to seeing her. Lucy had made a big chocolate layer cake, and Mom said they might as well take it straight to the barn because that's where the party was going to be.

"In that moldy old barn?" asked Lucy, and I could tell she didn't think much of the idea.

"It's what your brother wants." Mom shrugged her shoulders. "I couldn't stop him. He's got a big bonfire blazing in the middle. We'll be lucky if he doesn't burn everything up."

"No danger of that in this weather," declared Hank, untying his necktie and sticking it in his pocket. "I told you I didn't need this, Lucy. Come on, kids. This might be fun."

Sherry stayed behind with me. We were waiting for Nina Wachino, but before the Wachinos got there the Shaws and the Deans drove up. Mrs. Shaw had brought a huge potato salad and Mrs. Dean had made another cake, yellow with orange frosting. They both seemed to think the bonfire in the barn was a good idea. "Trust Simon to come up with something different," said Mrs. Shaw. And they went plowing through the backyard mud, giggling and laughing as though they were on their way to a real picnic.

The next car only stopped long enough to let Mildred Schultz out before it drove away. I watched her come slipping and sliding up the path and I felt like crying. Here I had to put up with her on the bus twice a day for five days a week, and now I was going to be stuck with her for the sixth.

"Who's that?" asked Sherry. "I never saw her before."

"She goes to my school. She's white. Simon invited her."

"That was nice of Simon," said Sherry. She's kind of dense sometimes, and she just heard the words, not the way I said them. "It was smart of her to wear galoshes, wasn't it?"

I could have told her that Mildred never went anywhere without galoshes from September until May. And that she always wore a fleece lined raincoat and a thick scarf covered with plastic over her head and usually carried an umbrella. But I didn't. Sherry would find out for herself.

Before Mildred had reached the porch, the Wachinos drove up. Mr. Wachino drives a log truck, and I guess he must make more money than Mr. Dean and Mr. Shaw, who work in the sawmill, because he gets a brand new car every year. They have four kids. The most important is Nina, who is fourteen, but her brother Ronnie is awfully cute, too. I wasn't sure Ronnie would come today because he's almost sixteen and doesn't stick around with his family much. He generally does things with his friends. But he was there. In fact, he was driving their new Buick.

They began piling out of the car as soon as it stopped, first the two little kids, then Mrs. Wachino, who carried something wrapped up in a dishcloth, then Nina and her father, and then Ronnie. Mildred kind of hesitated on the bottom step, but I called her up in a hurry. I wanted to introduce her to Mom and Sherry before the Wachinos got there. I was counting on Sherry to help me out with Mildred.

When the Wachinos arrive any place, it's sort of like a big tidal wave sweeping over everything. They all talk loudly and laugh loudly and kind of drown everything else out. Except Ronnie. He's quiet, and so good-looking that he doesn't have to make any noise to be noticed.

"I didn't know what to bring, Nancy," shouted Mrs. Wachino even before she was up the steps. "Because when Simon drove over to invite us I forgot to ask him what you planned to serve. So I brought spaghetti. It goes with almost everything, unless you're having Chinese food, and I didn't think you'd have that."

"Heavens no," said Mom quickly. "You didn't need to bring anything, Clara, but since you did spaghetti is wonderful."

"Were we supposed to bring something?" asked Mildred, straightening up from unbuckling her galoshes. "Nobody told me. I didn't bring anything."

"We didn't want you to," Mom assured her quickly. "Clara shouldn't have brought anything, either."

"You mustn't mind me, child," said Mrs. Wachino heartily. "I always take food wherever I go. It's a habit. I got a big family and we all eat a lot, so I always bring a little something extra. Sometimes I think people wish I wouldn't. My spaghetti probably isn't fit to eat anyway."

Mildred looked like she was going to cry, and I guess Mom wanted to distract her because she began introducing her around to all the Wachinos before I had to do it.

"Come on in. Don't stand out in the cold," she said the minute she'd finished saying names. And urged on by the wave of Wachinos, we all squeezed through the door.

"I don't think I've ever heard Plum mention you," Nina said to Mildred when we finally got to the kitchen.

"Hasn't she?" Mildred started unbuttoning her coat. "I talk about her all the time."

"Where is everybody?" shouted Mr. Wachino. "Where's the party?"

"In the barn," said Mom. Then she went on to explain about Simon's idea.

"Wow," said Ronnie and started for the door.

"Great stuff," approved Mr. Wachino. "Come on, kids."

"Put your coats back on," ordered Mrs. Wachino. "It may be chilly."

"It will be icy," agreed Mom. "We'll probably all have colds tomorrow."

"What a pretty dress," said Nina.

Mildred had finally struggled out of her coat. She was wearing a pink party dress with ruffles that made her look fatter than ever. I looked at Nina to see if she was being sarcastic, but she wasn't. In a way she was right. The dress was pretty, but not on Mildred.

"It's just the kind of dress I've always wanted," said Sherry.

Mildred's face got the color of her dress and she looked from Nina to Sherry. I'd never seen her smile like that before. It really changed her, made her look different. Somehow you almost forgot she was so fat when she smiled.

"It's old, really," she said finally. "But I've only worn it twice."

"Well, you be sure to fasten your coat up good to cover it before you go to the barn," advised Nina. "It would be a shame to get that dress dirty."

We all put on our coats and head scarfs and waited for Mildred while she squeezed into her galoshes again. Neither Nina nor Sherry seemed to see anything wrong with her. They just talked away, and didn't seem to notice that they had to wait a while until she could think of what to say before she answered. I wondered if they were being nice to her because they thought she was a friend of mine.

When we got to the barn everybody seemed to be having a good time in spite of the wind blowing through the cracks. Luckily it had stopped raining, so the roof wasn't leaking just then. The only ones who weren't right around the fire were the little kids. They were playing tag or some silly game with a lot of running that kept them warm. Nobody wanted to sit too close to Dave Beckett, even Grandma Longor, but he didn't seem to notice. He sat on the ground with his feet stretched out to the fire and smoked an old pipe that smelled as bad as he did. It wasn't tobacco he was smoking, but some kind of weed.

Pretty soon Mom came out carrying the roast venison and put it with the other food on the table made of boards across two sawhorses. She told me to go back and get the beans and sent Pop for the case of coke on the back porch.

When we came back only a few people were eating. The rest had strips of venison dangling from sticks over the fire.

"I've heard about this all my life," shouted Mr. Wachino. "But this is the first time I ever ate venison cooked like the old Indians did it."

"You don't have to eat it," Mom reminded him. "I cooked a roast, you know."

63

But nobody wanted the roast. Nobody had touched Dave Beckett's bucket of mussels and bay crabs either. Pretty soon he pulled it closer to where he was sitting, with a plate of spaghetti and beans on his lap. He fished a crab out of the pot and cracked it with his teeth. When he'd eaten the meat he threw the shell over his shoulder. Then he began on a mussel.

I looked at Grandma Longor, but I guess she hadn't noticed. Nina and Sherry had and they were giggling about it. Mildred was only staring with her popeyes, the way she always did.

"That looks like fun," she said after a minute. "Would he give me one?"

"Sure," agreed Sherry. "But I'd stick to the crab. Nobody but Dave Beckett would eat a mussel."

Mildred put down her plate and went over to Dave Beckett. I could see her lips move and he pointed to the kettle, inviting her to help herself. She sat down, reached in and pulled out a piece of crab. Then the most amazing thing happened. Ronnie Wachino walked over and took one too.

"Look at that," said Nina in disgust. "Ronnie's showing off again. Look, he's going to eat a mussel!"

"He's no worse than Mildred," I reminded her, wishing I'd been the one to try the shellfish.

"Of course he is," said Nina. "She's sticking to crab. Anybody can eat crab, but nobody but my brother and Dave Beckett would eat a mussel."

Mildred came back pretty soon and she was smiling. I'd have smiled too if Ronnie Wachino had come and sat down by me.

"That was fun," she told us. "Throwing shells.

You're supposed to throw them in a pile. Mr. Beckett says that throwing shells over your shoulder is called making a kitchen midden. But I felt like Henry VIII. I think I'll try cooking a piece of venison over the fire instead of another hot dog."

"I will too," said Sherry. "It can't be worse than a barbecue."

So we all tried cooking venison on a stick and it wasn't bad at all, after you'd salted it. In fact it was good enough so that Great-Grandma Lachance had to cut more strips, and the hot dogs just stayed on the table. Everybody ate and ate, and when we couldn't hold any more we just sat around the fire, feeling good and comfortable. Even the little kids quit running around and screaming like coyotes. While we were sitting there, Simon made a speech.

"Welcome to our potlatch," he said. "Thanks to the Lachances and Dave Beckett you got just a little sample of the way our ancestors celebrated a party."

"Let's hear it for the ancestors!" yelled Mr. Wachino and everybody cheered. I looked over at the bucket of mussels and bay crabs and couldn't believe my eyes when I saw that it was empty. Dave Beckett hadn't eaten all of them either. I'd seen other people besides Mildred and Ronnie cracking shells and throwing them on the pile.

"Of course there was more to a potlatch than just eating," continued Simon. "There was the giving of presents, and there was dancing. Grandma Lachance was telling me about the great times they used to have when the Warm House *tyee*—the chief—called a celebration in the old days. Our people came from the Siletz and the Grand Ronde both and camped for three days. Lots of food and games during the day and dancing most of the night."

Great-Grandma and Grandpa Lachance and Grandma Longor and Dave Beckett all nodded solemnly. You could almost see them remembering the good times they used to have.

"Those big gatherings in the Warm House were different from the powwows other tribes held across the mountains," said Simon. "We had two cultures on the Coast Reservation, the southern Oregon Indians who had horses and hunted game and made war, and the tribes along the coast and valley who built mighty canoes and used our rivers like we use the freeways today. They weren't strangers when the white man forced them onto the same reservation because once a year they'd meet at Wishram on the Columbia to trade. The Tutuntis, the Cayuse, the Nez Perce brought horses and dried buffalo meat that they'd crossed the Rockies to hunt. The Klamaths brought obsidian for arrowheads and Grandma Lachance tells me they brought slaves to sell as well. The Chinooks and their allied tribes brought fish, both fresh and dried into pemmican, and shells to be made into beads and wampum. So they knew each other when they arrived at the reservation, but they were suspicious, mistrustful. The only time they forgot that mistrust was when the Warm House tyee called them together."

Everybody was quiet. Even the Wachinos had stopped chattering and were listening.

"All those months I was in the hospital I had plenty of time to read and talk to people," said Simon. "And I found out that right now the Indian is very big. White people are interested in him, and it's paying off financially. Not from the government especially, but from the people themselves. In our own state, look at the Warm Springs in eastern Oregon. They've built a resort on their reservation. The whites come and shell out high prices to sleep in a luxury hotel just because it's run by Indians. Some of them pay to stay in a tepee and sleep on a cement floor. And their gift shops are doing a land-office business. They're showing the whites that the Indians had a culture of their own, a culture that had many things to recommend it. And besides that they're making money on the side. Why can't we get a little of that dough?"

"You forget, Simon, we're more white than Indian," pointed out Mr. Shaw. "We live like whites. We hold white man's jobs, and we draw white man's pay. Our kids go to white schools. There's not a person here who hasn't white blood, a lot of it. We're not reservation Indians like the Warm Springs, and we haven't been for years."

"Maybe so. But people still call us Indians, don't they?"

"Words never hurt nobody," pointed out Mr. Shaw stubbornly. "What does it matter what they call us so long as they let us alone? So long as I get my paycheck regular they can call me a cross-eyed goat. I don't care."

"But you do care," insisted Simon. "We all care.

Because the way a lot of the whites say the word 'Indian' it means 'second-class citizen.' "

I was surprised to hear him talk that way. After being such a big football hero in high school, I thought Simon was different.

"Well, it's the Indian's own fault. Some of them give the others a bad name," said Mrs. Dean, pursing up her lips like she'd bitten into a lemon. "You ever drive by skid road in Portland, Simon? And look at the bums panhandling on the street and sleeping it off in doorways. A lot of them bums are Indians. They're from important tribes, too, the ones you see on TV, not the one from around here. They're supposed to be Sioux and Apache and I don't know what all. I don't see why they have to come clear out here to carry on like that. They give the decent, law-abiding Indian a bad name."

"Not all the bums are Indian, are they Gloria?" asked Simon. "There's just as many whites along skid road."

"I suppose so," she admitted. "But the Indians stand out more. That's why I always tell Frank, a person can rise above what he was born to if he'll just keep his nose to the grindstone. Maybe people will forget it if he does that."

"There's nothing for them to forget," said Mr. Dean angrily. "I'm my own man. I stand on my own two feet. I'm not ashamed of being part Indian."

"But you don't have to wave it around like a flag, either," she told him.

I had the feeling that this wasn't a new argument at

68

their house. Mrs. Dean was all white, and every so often she'd throw it into the conversation so people wouldn't forget. To tell the truth, I didn't like her much, and I'm not sure anybody else did either. I don't know what color her hair had been to start with, but she bleached it and used a yellow dye. She always wore a lot of makeup and her clothes were just a little bit too tight where they shouldn't be.

"What's all this about making extra dough?" asked Mr. Wachino quickly, and I guessed he wanted to break up the argument before it got worse.

"Yeah," added Hank Pierce. "We can all use extra dough these days."

"What I want to do is show the whites the culture of our people," said Simon. "It's all but forgotten. Most of us here don't even remember. When Dave brought his bucket of shell fish and started a kitchen midden, what did we know about it? Gloria just said the Indians of the Pacific Northwest weren't important, but they were. Weren't they, Milo?"

"Yes, indeed," said Milo quickly. "The coast Indians made canoes so seaworthy that they took them whaling. Imagine spearing a whale from a canoe and following until the animal bled to death, then finally towing it back to shore! We didn't make totem poles here, like the Haidas and the Nootkas in the north, but we engaged in war with those tribes. Lewis and Clark did our people a great disservice when they reported in their journals that the Chinooks were lazy and dirty. The kitchen middens, where the shells were thrown, probably made the villages smell of fish, but the Chinooks and their allied tribes swam daily in the river. And they had no equal as boatmen."

"You want us to go whaling?" asked Hank, shaking his head. "Not me, brother."

I didn't blame him. The Pacific Ocean is nothing to fool around with.

"Of course not," said Simon impatiently. "We'll have to tell about that part. My idea is to hold a pot-latch once a week in the tourist season. We'll charge admission. Whites pay to attend Indian powwows and all they see is dancing. They're never invited to eat with the tribe afterwards. Sometimes whites pay tribes in Washington State to put on salmon bakes, and be-sides salmon the guests eat baked potato done up in aluminum foil, and blackberry pie, white man's food. At our potlatch we'll have only the food of our an-cestors, venison, which will have to be dried into jerky. Pemmican maybe. For you who don't know, that's dried fish and berries pounded and formed into cakes. Salmon, when we can get it. Shellfish, like we had today, and fruits in season or dried. If we could find them, *wapato* and *camas* would be good."

Nina nudged me and raised her eyebrows. I knew she was wondering what *wapato* and *camas* were. I wouldn't have known myself except that Milo had read about *wapato* in a book and told us. He said it was a tuber, kind of like a potato, that grew in marshy places. The Indian women used to dig it out with their bare feet and then bake it in the coals. Either they had dug it all out long before we were born or the places it grew had dried up because even Grandma Longor had never tasted *wapato*, although she'd heard about it.

70

She'd eaten *camas*, though. It was the bulb of a blue flower that looked a little like a hyacinth and grew in the meadows around here. When she was young, Grandma said, the fields were full of it and her mother gathered it every spring. Grandma said it was good to eat but it was easier to get things from the garden or the store than to go wandering all over digging bulbs out of the hard ground.

It took a few minutes for what he was saying to sink in. I couldn't believe it. Was Simon actually suggesting that we hold a potlatch for the whites and charge admission? I looked to see if he was joking, but he wasn't. He'd never been more serious in his life. He actually wanted us to dress up and sit on the ground and throw mussel shells over our shoulders. Well, if Simon thought Indians were second-class citizens now, by the time he got through we'd be fifth- or sixth-grade citizens.

"It would take an awful lot of food, Simon," said Mrs. Wachino. "And with prices the way they are, we might not even break even."

"Oh, we wouldn't buy anything. We'd scrounge it up ourselves. And we wouldn't try to fill anybody up either. Just a sample of everything, and a puff or two of the peace pipe when it was passed around. Do you know that isn't tobacco Dave is smoking? It's kinnikinic, and the woods are full of it. For free."

I hadn't noticed but Dave Beckett did have his horrible pipe going again. I wondered if there were bad effects from smoking kinnikinic.

"And there'd be dancing for entertainment," continued Simon enthusiastically. "Great-Grandma Lachance told me about the feather robe dance they used to have in the Warm House. I never heard of another tribe doing that. People dance singly, wearing a robe of feathers, and they keep time with the drums. If they lose a feather while they're dancing, they have to pay the Warm House tyee. The whites would love it. Whites like to bet, just as our people do."

"Maybe we could build a sweat house and show how the old timers used to cure sickness," said Milo thoughtfully.

"Why not?" asked Simon.

"Repulsive," said Mrs. Dean shuddering, and although I didn't like her I had to agree that she was right.

"Nobody remembers how to do those old dances, or how to build a sweat house," said Ronnie Wachino.

"I know," spoke up Dave Beckett, and Grandma Longor and the Lachances nodded that they remembered too.

"But if you do all those things, it's just like admitting —" began Mrs. Dean. Her husband jabbed her so hard in her ribs that she stopped talking.

"I could still make shell jewelry," volunteered Grandma Longor. "If somebody will get me the shells."

"Well, what do you think?" asked Simon. "You all had fun today. It would be like this once a week, only we'd charge our guests two bucks a head."

"I don't know," said Mr. Shaw. "Sounds like a lot of work to me. And we'd probably be expected to dress up in feathers and stuff. I'd feel like a fool."

"No feathers," corrected Milo quickly. "I've been

reading up on it. You'd wear a hat woven of straw that came up to a peak. The Tutuntis wore buckskin, but the Chinook men had robes of woodrat skin or a blanket fastened over one shoulder with a wooden pin. For war their women made them shirts of double thickness of deerhide that was said to be arrowproof."

"And arrowproof pants probably," added Ronnie. He seemed to be more enthusiastic than anyone, which surprised me a lot. I thought it was a horrible idea myself, and I didn't intend to have a thing to do with it.

"No pants," corrected Milo, smiling. "They didn't even wear a breach clout. Of course we couldn't go that far. We'll have to wear swim trunks at least, but there's no reason why they couldn't be dyed skin color."

"What did the women wear, Milo?" called Mrs. Wachino. "I'm always interested in fashions."

"Short petticoats of rushes or shredded bark," he told her. "And small bibs of rat skins, with shell and bead necklaces."

"Well, that certainly lets us out," declared Mrs. Dean. "I can't think of anything more repulsive."

"Of course, when you became a chief, costumes got a little more elaborate," continued Milo, as though he hadn't heard her. "Especially after the white man came. I read that Chief Concomely of the Chinooks wore an old gold-lace coat, a cocked hat and carried a sword and an old battered flag that some British sea captain gave him. And he only had one eye."

"Then maybe I'd better dress up and be Chief Concomely," said Simon, laughing. "I've only got one eye."

73

"You lie," accused Dave Beckett and his voice actually sounded a little scared. "You got two eyes."

"No, I don't." Simon touched his right eye gently with his finger. "See. I lost this in the war, and the army gave me a new one."

"Then you are Concomely," declared Dave, and this time you couldn't mistake his fear. "You come back. Always man come back to same family."

"You talk silly, Dave Beckett," Grandma told him. "Me, I'm a good Christian. Used to go to church every Sunday on the reservation. You talk like old blanket Indian. Simon's just Simon. He ain't Concomely."

"What does he mean?" asked Milo curiously.

"Old time Chinooks got fancy idea. Think dead come back after a while. Live again in body of somebody else," explained Great-Grandpa scornfully. Obviously the Tutuntis didn't share the belief. "Dave Beckett say Simon his own great-great-grandfather."

"Always some mark on body same as on old one," insisted Dave. "New baby have red mark on shoulder like grandfather. Black spot on face, maybe. Always the same."

"But I wasn't born with one eye. I lost it later," Simon reminded him.

"Same as great-great-grandfather," said Dave simply.

"What's all this about great-great-grandfather, anyway?" asked Milo. "What's he talking about?"

"Your ma was great-granddaughter or something of the old chief," explained Grandma Longor. "Don't mind Dave. He don't mean nothing. And anyway, there's nothing to be scared of. Simon wouldn't hurt a fly."

"Our mother, Sally Comely—Comely—Con-comely!" I could see that Milo was excited, but I didn't know why. The way he had described him, the old chief didn't sound too bright to me. But he and Simon looked at each other, grinning like a couple of coyotes.

"Why didn't you tell us, Grandma?" demanded Simon, but she only shrugged. It was so long ago I guess she didn't think it was important. Besides, Chief Concomely was not her ancestor.

"Fish-eaters always chop names. Lazy tongues." Great-Grandma Lachance looked at the rafters and appeared to be talking to herself. "My father called Tulumibigquata. Means 'Long Foot Bridge.' Never chop names. Bad luck."

"Sometimes it just happens," defended Grandma Longor angrily. "People say Longor to my man so much he become that."

"What was he before?" asked Milo quickly.

"Long Oar," Dave answered for her. "Your father's father—Frank Long Oar. His father's father"—he pointed to Mr. Wachino—"Watch-a-no. Watch-a-no mark paper for Clackamas tribe when they go on reservation."

"You mean my great-great-grandfather was a chief, too?" shouted Ronnie.

"Sure. Sure," his father told him. "But that's a long time ago, son. Like the old timers used to say, 'Many sleeps ago.' Nobody cares any more."

"I care," said Ronnie. "I care a lot. You should have told me."

"We're getting off the subject," pointed out Simon. "But do you see the possibilities? At the potlatch, the whites will get to meet and talk to descendents of men who were leaders of the first Americans. And instead of being second-class citizens, we'll be first class. That night, anyway. And we'll make a little extra money besides," he added, and I knew he was remembering that was the suggestion that got their attention in the beginning.

"What makes you think anybody would want to meet us?" asked Mr. Shaw. "So far nobody's been breaking down my door trying to make my acquaintance."

"Right now there's a lot of interest in the Indian and sympathy for him," explained Simon.

"Not where I work," said Mr. Shaw. "You do your job and you get paid. It's as simple as that. It's the kind of work you turn in that counts."

"You mean you've never had sombody call you Mr. Tommy Hawk?" asked Mr. Dean.

"If they do, I don't listen."

"Me neither," said Mr. Wachino. "Not that many people would. There's something to be said for weighing over two hundred fifty pounds."

"You're all missing the point," interrupted Ronnie angrily. "Simon's trying to do something for our people and you won't listen."

"We're listening, son," said Mr. Wachino mildly.

"Where would you have this potlatch?" inquired Mr. Shaw suspiciously. "You'd have to have a building of some kind."

"That's going to be our biggest problem," admitted Simon. "But we'll face it later. First, let's see how many of you want to go in on it. Frank?"

"No," decided Mr. Dean after a few noticeable nudges from his wife. "Count me out, Simon. I'm satisfied with things the way they are."

"Okay," said Simon. "Hank?"

Hank grinned and said he'd go along if it didn't interfere with the fishing season. We all understood that, because he had to make a living. We knew why he'd said yes, too. Lucy would have skinned him alive if he'd disappointed her brother, Simon.

"Mr. Shaw?"

"I just couldn't bring myself to wrap up in a blanket out in public, Simon," he admitted sheepishly.

"Mr. Wachino?"

Mr. Wachino said he was looking forward to a busy season. He could get time and a half overtime driving his truck, and he didn't think the admissions from any potlatch would make up for that.

"I will," said Ronnie as soon as his father stopped speaking. "I think it's great."

When I heard that I decided I wouldn't kick up a fuss. Not in the beginning, anyway. I was pretty sure the whole thing would fall through eventually.

"Good boy," said Simon.

Dave Beckett and Grandma Longor both agreed to do anything they could to help with the potlatch, but the Lachances lived too far away.

"Except for *mowitch*," said Great-Grandpa. "I get you all you want of that."

"Dry it up first, will you?" asked Simon. "Grandma Lachance knows how. I still remember her jerky from when I was a little boy."

From the way Great-Grandma looked at Grandma Longor, sort of gloating, I knew we'd have jerky coming out our ears.

"The way I count that makes nine adults and six kids," said Simon. "I'm counting Ronnie Wachino as an adult. We ought to be able to put on a pretty fair potlatch with that." He paused, frowning just a little. "Yes, Mildred. What is it?"

I hadn't noticed but now I saw that she was waving her hand in the air the way little kids in school do when they want to be called on.

"You forgot me," she explained. "You asked everybody but me, and I want to help with the potlatch."

"But Mildred, you're not an Indian. Your people were German."

It had finally come, the moment I had been waiting for. Now everybody would see how stupid Mildred really was. I couldn't even feel sorry for Simon, although I knew how hard it was to argue her down once she'd made up her mind about something.

"That's not my fault," she insisted stubbornly. "Couldn't you make an exception? Let me be an associate member or something?"

"We'll do better than that," he told her, grinning suddenly. "We'll make you an official blood sister of the tribe, Mildred."

Honestly, I just wanted to die.

Simon took Great-Grandma and Grandpa Lachance home on Sunday and came back the same day. It was only a little over an hour's drive but I guess the long walk on rough ground in and back from the cabin must have tired him. When he got home he went to bed and stayed there for two days. He joked about it and said the deerskin he brought back for Grandma Longor to sew into the foundation of a feather cape was so heavy it strained his back. It didn't. Even Andy could carry it. It seemed funny to think of Simon, who used to be able to hold his own in a wrestling match with Pop, getting tired. But he said it was because he'd just got out of the hospital and that

79

laying around hospitals made anybody soft. I've never been in one but Milo has and he didn't say anything, so I guess it's true.

Pop went back to work in the woods on Monday and I went back to school. It was just the same as before except that Mildred talked more on the bus. Every day she asked me if Simon had found a place to hold the potlatch yet and every day I said no. Personally, I didn't think he'd ever find one. At least I hoped he wouldn't. I didn't want my family making a spectacle of themselves.

It was next to impossible to find the right building. In the first place, it had to be at one of the beach towns so it would be easy for the tourists to come. They wouldn't drive up some back road like the one to Cooperville. It had to be right under their noses. Then the building had to have a roof because it rains a lot at the beach, even in summer. It had to be one big, open room, like our barn, where benches could be built around the sides, but most buildings were cut up into small rooms. And Simon said we had to build a fire in the middle of the floor. No fire marshal would stand for that, to say nothing of the owner of the building. I figured we were perfectly safe. I didn't think there was a building like that on the whole coast. But I guess I was the only one who felt like that because the others started getting ready.

Pop had brought home loads of cedar bark for Grandma to shred into skirts as soon as she finished the feather cape. That cape was really something. The foundation was thin deerskin and it was covered with chicken feathers. The feathers had to be sewed just right, not too tight and not too loose. If they were too loose the dancer would lose them all at once, then there would be no challenge. But Simon hoped some of them would come off because we would make money every time a feather dropped. He and Pop took turns dancing in the cape every night. It was tricky. But if they were very careful and didn't twitch too much, they could get through the whole dance without losing a single feather.

Milo was going to be one of the drummers since he could do that sitting down, and he practiced every day. Smelly old Dave Beckett, who was the other drummer, came over and taught him the proper beats and the chants they were supposed to sing. When Milo wasn't practicing on the drum or working at the library, he carved little wooden animals to sell at the table with the baskets and arrowheads. His disposition had changed since Simon had come home and he wasn't nearly so grouchy as he used to be. He hardly ever yelled at the little boys any more, and, when he was pounding his drum or whittling, the good side of his mouth turned up a little, as though he was thinking of something nice.

Pop and Simon and the little boys had gone to the beach on a couple of low tides and come home with buckets of shells, everything from clams and mussels to periwinkles. They boiled them to take out the smell, and from the little ones Grandma said she'd make jewelry. The larger ones would be plates to put food on. Clams and mussels aren't very big. They'd only hold a bite or two, but Simon said that was all we'd serve of each thing, just a taste.

Only Mom and I were doing nothing to get ready. Mom said she was too tired when she got home at night, and I didn't think it was worthwhile. I thought it was a shame to do all this work for nothing, but at least it gave my family something to think about.

The days were beginning to get a little longer now, and you could tell spring was coming. The sky was still gray and heavy with rain, but there was a different smell in the air. The grass seemed to be a little greener than it had been, and gray pussy willows popped out on brown branches that you would have sworn were dead. The mountain snow began to melt under the warmer rains and it rushed down in little streams, leaving lakes of muddy water which stood in some of the fields.

Mildred kept on asking if we'd found a place for the potlatch, only now she began harping on something else as well. She wanted me to come to her house for dinner.

I didn't want to go, even though I was a little curious about how her house looked inside, so I kept saying I couldn't. I had a good excuse. Grandma Longor always had chores for me when I got home from school.

Then one Saturday, Mildred knocked at our front door. Andy let her in and brought her straight to the kitchen.

I was cleaning the stove, which I didn't like to do, and everything was a mess. If it had been anybody else but Mildred Schultz I would have been humiliated to death.

"Hi, Mildred," I said. "Did you want something?"

She stared at me, then she shook her head. "No," she said after a minute. "I came to see your grandmother."

Grandma's eyes popped open wide. Nobody ever comes to see her.

"Set down," she said. "Set in rocking chair."

"I can't stay. My poppa is waiting in the car," Mildred told her slowly. "Mrs. Longor, I came to ask if Plum can come to my house for Sunday dinner tomorrow."

"Plum? Eat at your house?" Grandma looked at her sharply.

"I ate with her," insisted Mildred. "My folks say it is time to repay her hospitality. I've asked her before, but she always has chores. Maybe Sunday is different."

I knew, even before she spoke, what Grandma would say. She doesn't believe in being beholden to anyone. What Mildred said made sense to her. Mildred ate here at Simon's potlatch. It was my turn to eat at her house.

"Tomorrow very good day," said Grandma approvingly. "Plum come to your house to eat."

So the next day I had to go to the Schultzes' for dinner.

Simon drove me over and Mildred must have been watching because she had the front door open before I'd climbed the porch steps. Her parents were right behind her, and the way they were both smiling I guess they were glad I'd come.

Mrs. Schultz looked younger than her husband. She had lots of blond hair, like Mildred, only her braids were wound around her head. She was short and pretty fat, but it didn't look funny on her. It just made her look jolly. She wore a blue-and-white checked dress and an embroidered white apron, and when Mildred introduced us she gave me a big hug. She smelled of good things like spices and sugar and vanilla and soap and raspberries.

Mildred had told me to come at one o'clock, and Mrs. Schultz said dinner wasn't going to be until three but that we could have a little snack to hold us until then. So we went right out to the kitchen where she poured the biggest glasses of milk I ever saw and brought out a full plate of cookies. The milk was half cream and the cookies were so rich I could only eat two, but Mildred ate five and filled her milk glass the second time. Then she wanted me to see her room.

When we went through the house to go upstairs I noticed how clean everything was. The furniture and rugs were nice, as nice as you'd expect the second richest man in town to own, but the sparkle and shine was what you saw first. There wasn't a bit of lint anywhere or a single vase or ornament out of place. Mrs. Schultz must have spent a lot of time cleaning.

Mildred's room was blue and fluffy. There was a ruffled blue bedspread and blue ruffled curtains at the windows. The rug on the floor was blue, and the furniture white with wreaths of blue forget-me-nots painted on it. Like the rest of the house, it was so clean it made me uncomfortable, and when I sat in a round blue upholstered chair, I hoped there wasn't any mud on my clothes.

"My parents like you," said Mildred. "They wanted to like you because you are my friend. Now they have met you they like you for yourself."

"They're very nice." It made me feel funny to have her talk like that, as though I'd just passed a test of some kind. "I think your mother's pretty, too."

"I don't look like my mother." Mildred sounded sad, and I couldn't help feeling sorry for her. "I look like my father."

It was true, so I didn't try to deny it. I just smiled and waited for her to bring up another subject. I couldn't think of one myself. It was hard to talk to Mildred.

"If I looked like my mother maybe I would have more friends," she said finally. "I only have one friend, Plum. You."

"That's not true," I denied, but I kind of figured it was so. She hadn't had any friends at Cooperville Elementary and she hadn't seemed to make any at Sunset. "Nina and Sherry liked you that day at our house, remember? They'd probably be your friends if they had a chance."

"What a day!" Mildred's eyes shone as she remembered. I felt guilty because I hadn't wanted her there. "They're nice girls."

I nodded, wishing she would talk about something else but she didn't.

"Will you show me how to make people like me, Plum?"

"Me?" I couldn't believe I was hearing right. "Me show you how to make the kids like you? I'm the last person in the world to know how to do that. Nobody likes me. You've seen how they treat me on the bus."

"But that's your own fault," she said after a long wait. "You always look so angry you scare people. All but me. I know you are good inside. When somebody speaks to you, you chop your words off hard when you answer, like you wanted to bite the one who spoke to you."

I stared at her, feeling my face get red. I didn't do those things, and anyway who did she think she was to say so?

"It's true, Plum," she told me, and I thought for a minute she was going to cry.

"All right then. The reason why the kids don't like you is that you're so fat," I said angrily. "And that's because you eat too much. Why just a few minutes ago you had five cookies and two glasses of milk. And pretty soon you'll eat a big dinner. Where do you think it's going to go? To fat, that's where."

She didn't get mad, the way I expected her to. Instead she went to the dressing table and looked at herself in the mirror.

"My mother is fat," she said finally. "You said she was pretty."

"It's different in old people. When you get old you can get as fat as you want. But now you should be thin." I went over to stand beside her and when I saw myself in the glass I did look angry. But that was because of what she'd said. I didn't look that way all the time. Or did I?

"I'll go on a diet," said Mildred, "if you'll learn how to smile."

It struck me so funny I broke down laughing. She laughed too, and then she did change the subject. She asked if I wanted to play some of her new records. She had my favorites and a lot I'd never heard, so we listened until Mrs. Schultz called us to dinner.

It was a wonderful dinner. Mrs. Schultz cooked as well as she cleaned. There was some kind of meat they called *wiener schnitzel*, only it didn't have wienies in it, covered with gravy and served with noodles and boiled potatoes and broccoli with a cheese sauce and carrots and peas swimming in butter and hot biscuits. For dessert there was cooked fruit on a pastry, all smothered in whipped cream. I'd never tasted such food in my life.

Mr. and Mrs. Schultz kept urging me to have more, but finally I was up to my neck and couldn't swallow another bite.

"A fair dinner you ate," said Mrs. Schultz, beaming. Then she turned to Mildred and her pink face puckered with disapproval. "But you! You ate nothing. A bite or two of your *wiener schnitzel*, and you pushed off the gravy. A little vegetable. No dessert. What is this? Are you coming down sick?"

"No, Mama," Mildred told her. "I'm on a diet. Tomorrow, please don't butter the vegetables till they get to the table."

Then she looked at me, and I smiled back so wide I could feel the creases in my cheeks.

After that day, we got along a lot better. I didn't

87

even mind when Mildred brought her lunch over to my table at school and ate with me. In a way it was nice, because I'd always eaten alone and so had she. I could tell she was trying to lose weight because all she had in her lunch sack were carrots and celery, but I guess her fat had been on a long time because it was slow to budge.

"Maybe there's something wrong with my glands," she said one day. "I only lost two pounds."

"You've had a checkup and the doctor says your glands are fine," I reminded her. "Besides, I can't see any changes in me either. I go around smiling like the Cheshire cat and nobody notices."

"It takes time." There was hardly any pause before she answered. Maybe the diet wasn't doing much to help Mildred's weight, but something was making her speak up quicker than she ever had. At least when we were alone.

The weeks slipped by. Mildred kept losing pounds on the scales even though they hardly showed on her, and some of the kids I hadn't known before in Sunset began speaking to me in the halls. The Cooperville crowd was just the same, but we both felt a little better about it because now there were two of us.

Then one day Mildred got on the bus and squashed down beside me. Her blue eyes, which I didn't notice as being popped out any more, were twinkling.

"I know a secret," she announced.

"What?"

But she wouldn't tell. All she would say was, "You'll find out tonight."

She wouldn't tell at noon either, although I tried to get her to. She just kept twinkling and smiling and saying that I'd find out later.

I did, too, the minute I got home from school. There were Simon, Grandma and the little boys actually doing some kind of a war dance around the kitchen floor while Milo sat in his chair, beating on his drum.

"Here's Plum! Tell her!" shrieked Chris.

"We got it, Plum," yelled Andy.

"Got what?" I asked, staring at them. Whatever it was, it was something they wanted. Everyone was grinning so wide it's a wonder their mouths didn't split.

"A place to have our potlatch," Simon told me. "Your friend Mildred kept nagging at her uncle until he agreed to let us use an old storage barn at Cannon Beach. It's got a concrete floor and walls, and it's close to the tourists. We're all set!"

"Good," I said and sat down because my knees felt rubbery. "Good for Mildred," I added, but I didn't mean it at all.

There was a practice for everybody who was going to be in the potlatch the next Sunday afternoon. It was in our barn because Simon said we needed a lot of rehearsals before anybody could see us. I'd watched Indians dancing on TV and I didn't think we'd need much practice. People just hopped around in a circle and every once in a while they'd give a whoop or a holler. It didn't look like much, and I didn't want to make a fool of myself. But I decided I'd go along with the rehearsal anyway because Ronnie Wachino was coming. Maybe after they got to doing it, everybody would feel as silly as I did and they'd call the whole thing off.

Even though it was April by now and the pussy willows had yellow fuzz over their gray fur, it was raining. It rains a lot in Oregon, especially at the beach. People get used to it, but when we go inside we don't expect the rain to follow us. It did in the barn. Some of the leaks in the roof were bigger than ever, and the water came down like somebody had left a faucet running. Pop laid a big fire in the center of the driest spot and we were supposed to dance around that.

Ronnie Wachino was the first one there on Sunday. He had just had his sixteenth birthday and he drove up on a brand new Honda that his folks had given him for a present. He got there at ten in the morning, and the rehearsal wasn't supposed to start until one.

When Mom saw him coming up the path she said, "What are we going to do with that boy for three hours?" But Simon said he was glad Ronnie had come early. It proved that he had a lot of enthusiasm and a sense of his tribal heritage, which was a lot more than could be said for most of the adults around here.

Of course the little boys were terribly excited about the Honda and Ronnie took them each for a ride. I don't think they went very far because they weren't gone long. When they came back, red-cheeked and burbling, Ronnie asked if I didn't want a ride too.

"You'll have to put your jeans back on," said Mom even before I had a chance to answer. I'd run upstairs and changed into a dress the minute I saw Ronnie coming up the path.

"Why'd you put on your school dress anyway?"

asked Grandma, scowling. "School dresses for school days."

"My jeans are dirty," I said. I didn't remind them there was a big tear on the knee of one pair and the other was so tight I couldn't zip it clear to the top.

"Who cares about a little dirt?" asked Ronnie. "Look at me. Mud splashes up your legs when you go over rough roads. Might as well start out dirty because you'll end up that way anyway."

I wanted to go more than anything. Not that I wanted to ride on a Honda. It was just that Ronnie Wachino had asked me. But I hated to have him see my knee sticking out of my jeans. It looked so sloppy. I'd have had time to mend them if he hadn't come so early.

"Go on," said Simon, giving me a push. "Change your clothes. You can wear my jacket if you want to. It will be too big for you, but you can roll up the sleeves. The wind will really whip around."

Well, that settled it. Simon had bought himself some new clothes, and he had a red jacket lined with white furry stuff. It was as light as dandelion fluff, but as warm as the fire in the cookstove. Since it would be too big, it might even come down to my knees. I rushed upstairs to change.

The jacket didn't cover the tear in my knee, but the color was very becoming. I could tell when I peeked into Mom's mirror. Maybe Ronnie would be so busy looking at Simon's jacket he wouldn't notice my jeans.

Ronnie didn't say anything about either the jacket or the jeans. We went outside in the rain, and he handed me a heavy plastic helmet that snapped under the chin.

"I know these are a drag," he told me. "But in Oregon you got to wear them. It's the law."

I put on the helmet and after he straddled the new Honda I climbed on behind the way he showed me.

"I thought we'd go down to the beach," he said. "There won't be anybody else there in this rain and the tide's out. It's a chance to really open her up."

Then he pushed down with his heel a couple of times and the engine began to roar. Roar was the right word. We couldn't hear each other talk, not that there was anything I wanted to say. I was too scared to open my mouth. I'd never liked Hondas, even when other people rode them and I was safely on the ground. I hung on as tight as I could, and I didn't even think it was Ronnie Wachino I was hanging onto. I shut my eyes and felt the wind whistle past and when the Honda went over bumps in the road I felt myself rise out of the seat for a second and hit it again a second later. I clamped my teeth and hung on, without even bothering to ask myself why I had ever got into this mess in the first place.

It felt like hours and hours, but I guess it couldn't have been more than twenty or thirty minutes later before the torture came to an end. The roaring stopped. We were standing still.

"Look at that!" Ronnie's voice sounded thin with only the background of the ocean behind it. "The beach is full of logs! Must have been a big storm to wash so many up."

I opened my eyes and we were on the bluff looking down on Short Sands Beach. As Ronnie said, a storm had filled it almost full with huge logs. Only a few had pieces of bark still clinging to them. Most were scoured smooth and gray by the sea. I'd never paid much attention to the big logs that wash up after a storm, but I was sure glad to see those. If I had been close enough, I'd have kissed them.

"What a shame." I could hear my voice trembling, and I couldn't help it.

"Hey," said Ronnie in a concerned tone. "Don't take it so hard. I didn't know you were so crazy about bikes. My sister Nina's a real chicken. You wouldn't catch her on the back of a Honda. I'm glad you're not like her."

"I've never been on one before," I said honestly. Now that we were on the ground, I was beginning to get my courage back.

"I suppose we could go down to Cannon," said Ronnie thoughtfully. "But we'd probably find logs there, too. And at Seaside the beach patrol wouldn't let us open up the way we want to."

I nodded gratefully.

"Tell you what," he decided. "I'm hungry. We passed a hamburger joint back there a ways. What do you say we get a burger and decide what to do?"

"Great idea," I told him quickly. "How far is it?"

"Not far. Right on the highway. Didn't you see it when we passed?"

"I must have been thinking of something else."

"Your first ride on a Honda does that for you,"

Ronnie agreed. "It's like nothing in this world. Maybe flying's better. I wouldn't know about that, but someday I'll find out."

We climbed back on, and I hoped he was right about the diner being only a little way. Since it was on the paved highway, our ride was smoother than the graveled road into Cooperville. I even managed to open my eyes a crack and watch the world go whirling past.

The diner was just a Mama-and-Papa grocery store with one counter. The owners lived in back and they cooked hamburgers and hot dogs in their own kitchen. In the summer they may have had a take-out trade, but today we were the only customers. We sat on stools and Ronnie ordered two hamburgers and cokes.

The man, who was kind of grumpy, went back to make them and while he was doing it Ronnie told me all about his new Honda. I didn't listen to what he was saying because I wouldn't have understood it anyway. I just heard his voice and watched his face. He was the handsomest boy I'd ever seen. And this was the very first time in my whole life a boy had taken me out for a hamburger. I thought how nice it would be if we could get to be friends and I could ask him to the carnival dance at Sunset High next year. Mary Beth and the other Cooperville girls would really sit up and take notice of Ronnie Wachino, even if he was an Indian.

The man brought our hamburgers and cokes and collected for them right away. Then he went back into his own part of the building.

95

"You know," said Ronnie, "I'm sure glad your brother Simon came home."

I guessed he was through talking about engines and carburetors so I began to listen.

"So am I," I agreed. "He was gone a long time."

"It did him good, though. He got out to see the world, away from this coast. I hope he'll be able to make a go of this potlatch thing. People like my dad need to be jolted out of their little ruts. Do you know, he never reads a newspaper? Once in a while he looks at news on television, but he doesn't have any idea of what's going on outside. And everybody else around here is just like him."

"What do you mean?" I asked carefully. I wasn't too sure what Ronnie was talking about. It was almost as bad as his Honda talk.

"Why, the Indian movement," he told me seriously. "All over the country it's going on. Those guys that used to be at Alcatraz and at Wounded Knee, every place! All this was our land to begin with, every acre of it! The white man just moved in and took it, and gave us piddling little patches of worthless ground in exchange. It's time we stood up for our rights. We've got to show them we're here and we mean to have our share."

"Some of it wasn't such bad land." I felt I had to say something because Ronnie was looking at me as though I should.

"A few tribes lucked out," he admitted. "Oklahoma, maybe, because they had oil. But they wouldn't have had that land if the whites had known it was there.

Not many tribes did so well. Look at us, for instance. We got mostly timber and undeveloped land. As soon as the white man saw the possibilities and the price of lumber went up, they dissolved the reservation and bought us out for peanuts."

"But Grandma said most of the Indians had moved off the reservation by then." I remembered her saying it, and Pop had agreed.

"Sure," he agreed promptly. "Because people like your dad and mine were stupid. They didn't know enough to hang on until the price was right. They tried to make themselves into white men, and that can't be done. At least, it shouldn't be done. Not until we get what's coming to us."

"Do you think Simon's potlatch is going to help?" I didn't see how it could.

"I admit it's not much, but it's a beginning," Ronnie said gravely. "It will let the white man know we're around. It will bind us together. In unity there's strength, like the man said. Maybe we can get back some of what's coming to us."

"I don't see how we can," I said helplessly.

"That's because you're a girl," he told me smugly. "But you're a smart kid. You're not like my sister, Nina. All she thinks about is how she looks and what people think of her. That's why she wouldn't go along with the potlatch. But you did! This is the first step, just a little step, mind you, to get us recognition. When I saw you were for it, I knew there was hope for you. All you need is to be steered in the right direction. You're smart enough to listen to your elders.

If I didn't think so I wouldn't waste my time talking to you."

"I'm not a kid," I told him angrily. "I'll be fourteen in two months."

"That's still a kid," Ronnie reminded me. "I was sixteen last week."

He began eating his hamburger, but I could only nibble at mine. Ronnie Wachino thought I was just a kid, and no matter what he said I wasn't sure he believed I was very smart. He was just hoping to get me to think the way he did, and I didn't like it.

I was so mad at Ronnie that I don't even remember much about the rehearsal. Every time she had a chance, Mildred kept whispering to me to smile, but I didn't pay any attention. If she'd been through what I had, she wouldn't smile either.

There was more to an Indian dance than I had thought. There was a funny little shuffling step that you could do either fast or slow according to the drum beat, but I caught on right away when Grandma showed us. I was awfully glad that Ronnie didn't. He had to be shown several times, which proved he would have been a terrible dancer and it's a good thing I hadn't invited him to the carnival at Sunset. Imagine spending an evening with somebody who couldn't keep time to the music!

That night I went to bed early and Simon did too. The next morning he told us he had to go into the Veteran's Hospital in Portland for a checkup. He said he was supposed to do that every few months and there was nothing to worry about. So we didn't. He said he'd be back in plenty of time for next Sunday's rehearsal.

When I got home the next afternoon, Grandma wasn't there. This was very unusual because she never goes any place. Milo said she was out digging roots.

"What does she want with roots?" I asked. Nobody digs roots unless they're clearing ground for a garden.

"For the potlatch. There are certain kinds of roots that can be cooked with squirrel or rabbit into stew. Her mother used to do it. Pop's going to shoot a few rabbits and Grandma's going to cook them up the way the old Indians did."

That potlatch again!

"Yuk!" I told him. I couldn't think of anything worse. "How's she going to keep them till next summer? Meat spoils."

"In the Schultz's freezer," Milo said, grinning with the good side of his mouth. "Don't you remember yesterday when Grandma was talking about rabbit stew and your friend Mildred offered to store it for her? Grandma still doesn't believe it can be done. I guess she never heard of freezers. But Simon and I convinced her. It has to be made now because by summer these particular roots would be too tough."

That must have been part of yesterday's rehearsal that had gone over my head, but I just grunted and let it go. It was too bad, I thought, that Mildred Schultz and I couldn't change places. She was so interested in the potlatch she should have been the Indian.

Mildred's diet was beginning to show some results. She could put her whole hand inside her waistband and wiggle her fingers, and she said she'd lost ten pounds. She was having better luck than I was, providing she was right about me, which I still wasn't ready to concede. I really didn't believe I went around scowling. Anyway, there wasn't much to smile about these days. All my family thought about and talked about was the potlatch, and I was fed up with it.

Grandma had finished the feather cape and now she was making shredded bark skirts. If you were willing to call them Hawaiian skirts, they wouldn't have been so bad because that's what they looked like. But nobody would. They called them Chinook skirts. We were going to wear sleeveless bodyshirts under them that Mom had dyed to match our skin. And instead of pretty Hawaiian flower leis, we had fur bibs from the rabbits Pop had killed for the stew. I thought they were hideous.

Lucy was weaving the hats for the men and sewing the blankets they would wear over their brown shorts so at least I didn't have to push them off chairs every time I wanted to sit down or look at them hanging from nails on the wall. That was one blessing.

I wanted to get out of the whole thing, but I didn't know how. Everybody took it for granted that I felt like they did even when I was grumpy. At rehearsals, Sherry and Mildred went out of their heads with excitement and that dumb Ronnie Wachino kept grinning at me and saying, "Atta girl," until I wanted to scream. Even Mom was beginning to get a little worked up to it by this time. Maybe Simon guessed I wasn't too happy since he gave me a spot where I danced by myself because everybody said I was the best dancer. But it didn't make me feel any better. I wished I had the nerve to tell them what I really thought, but I didn't.

One Saturday after we had the dance part pretty well whipped into shape, Simon asked if I wanted to take a ride with him.

"Where?"

"Just around. Maybe up in the hills. The snow's cleared out now, and I'd like to see the mountains again."

The little boys wanted to go too, but this time Simon said no. He said he wanted to spend a few hours alone with me. They'd get their turns later. It was kind of a funny thing for him to say, but I was glad. Simon and I hadn't had much time alone since he got back.

May is a wonderful month in our part of the country. Sometimes it gets really warm, and the air smells of blossoms and fresh-turned dirt from people's gardens. You can hear bees buzzing around while they pop into flowers to see what flavor each is, and birds keep twittering away as they finish their nests. You forget all about the early June rains, and you think summer is really here.

Simon drove up an old logging road into the mountains. Higher up on the peaks there were a few splotches of snow that hadn't melted, but there wasn't any along the road. The fir trees looked tall and green against the blue sky, and here and there little white faces of trilliums were peeking out from their green leaves or there'd be tiny lavender spring beauties or lambs-tongues. All the brown switches and brush had come alive with green leaves, and every fallen log was covered with wild blackberry vines. I told myself I must remember this place. Real wild blackberries were getting harder and harder to find. The seedy evergreens were choking them out, but this was one spot where they still grew.

"You like it up here, don't you, Plum?" said Simon. "I can tell because you're smiling. The little girl I left when I went away used to smile all the time. The one I came home to almost never does."

I didn't know what to say so I didn't say anything. Maybe Mildred was right after all. Maybe I did go around scowling. But I didn't mean to.

"You know, I used to dream about this place, or places like it, all those months in the hospital," said Simon after a minute. I was glad he was going to drop the subject of my not smiling. "Up here it's just like it used to be when our forefathers lived in these forests."

"I thought Milo said Indians didn't live in the forests, only in clearings," I reminded him. Every evening Milo had been giving us little lectures on our early ancestors. Some of the things were interesting, but a lot was just dumb.

"They came here whenever they found an animal trail to follow," insisted Simon. "That old saw about Indians finding their way through strange forests is bunk. One fir tree looks like a dozen other fir trees. It's easy to get lost."

I nodded and took a long sniff of the air. It really smelled good, the bitey tang of fir, the sweetness of wild flowers and the scent of earth drying out after the winter. Somewhere nearby there must be a little mountain stream because I could hear it trickling down the slope.

"I wanted to thank you for being in the potlatch, Plum," said Simon after a while. "Sometimes I don't think you really want to, and I know you're doing it to please me. I really appreciate it."

I looked at him quickly to see if he were being sarcastic, but he wasn't. He was just smiling, the way only Simon could smile, and I knew he meant it.

"That's all right," I said. I didn't know what else to say. I couldn't tell him what I really thought.

"This potlatch is pretty important to me," he continued. "I've been thinking about it all those months in the hospital, not the potlatch itself, but something that would bring our people together."

"Why do you want to do that?" I asked cautiously.

"Heritage maybe. I don't know. I just thought it ought to be done. The whites do it all the time, brag about their English, or Scandinavian, or French ancestry. They bring their customs out and make a lot of them, like the Scandinavians' smorgasbord, or the English plum pudding."

104

"I don't think eating raw mussels and throwing the shells over your shoulder will ever get popular," I told him.

"I don't think so, either." Simon laughed. "But other customs might. The main idea is that we've got to learn to be proud of our Indian blood, not hide it."

"Why?"

"Because it's the only way we can get over being second-class citizens." Simon was very serious all of a sudden. "If we look on ourselves as that, other people will too. We've got to respect ourselves before we can expect the world to respect us. Look what the blacks have done. They kept saying 'black is beautiful' so often, they made the rest of us believe it too. Our people didn't go at it that way. A lot of us moved off the reservation and tried to make ourselves white."

"You mean we should have stayed on the reservation until we could get more money for our land?" I wondered if he believed the way Ronnie did.

Simon stared at me a minute, then he laughed.

"No. I'm not a revolutionary and I'm not an advocate of Red Power. I just want my people, my tribe, to hold up their heads and take pride in being what they are."

"How can the potlatch do that?"

"By showing the people, our people as well as the whites, that the Indian had a culture of his own. That his life didn't consist of running around waving tomahawks and painting his face for war. We survived in a wilderness, unassisted by the white world. Maybe the whites wouldn't have done as well as we did. We'll never know about that. We made our own tools, provided adequate shelter, manufactured clothing, found food and made our own entertainment. We had our own laws and religion. We have nothing to be ashamed of. The potlatch is one of our ancient customs, and I want you to remember, Plum, that we're not doing it only for the whites who will come to see it. We're doing for ourselves, to remind us of our forefathers. That's why I'm so glad you're going along with it, even though I have a hunch you don't think much of the idea."

"Oh, it's all right," I said weakly. What could I say?

But after that I couldn't tell him what I really thought of his potlatch. And I couldn't try to get out of it either. I had to go along and pretend I liked it.

School was always out early in June and right afterwards the tourists started flocking to the beach. It didn't give us too much time to get ready for them.

Pop started making benches to go across two sides of the cement warehouse but he could only work weekends. Simon helped him, and when Perry Schultz found out about it he showed up to help, too. It's a good thing he did, because they were getting low on lumber and Perry got them a discount. Even second-grade lumber is expensive, and Simon said it would eat a hole in our profits to pay for it. I guess Perry must have been a pretty good carpenter because the two of them finished the job without waiting for Pop.

107

Perry must have thought it was fun because when the benches were finished he kept trying to think of other things he could do. He said we should have a big sign, something to attract attention, on the outside of the building and he brought over a real Navajo blanket to hang. When Simon explained that the Coast Indians didn't have Navajo blankets, he suggested a totem pole. Simon said that wouldn't work either. Oregon and Washington Indians didn't make totem poles, only the tribes farther north. Then Perry wanted to know what they did have, and when Simon said canoes he asked how about the one in our barn.

So he and Simon hung the one-man canoe that Milo had whittled out of a cedar log up over the street. I guess it was hard to do and Simon said he wanted to give up several times, but Perry kept at it. It really did look good when they finally got it up and it certainly attracted attention.

Simon said Perry could go with him to get the baskets, arrowheads and jerky from Great-Grandma and Grandpa Lachance, but Milo reminded him how tired he had got the last time he made that trip in one day. They argued about it so much that finally Pop put his foot down and said he was tired of listening to them. He'd go himself, and if he heard any more about it he'd go out and get drunk. Simon gave in when he heard that because he knew Pop meant it. He hadn't touched a drop since Simon got home, but I knew he was itching to and that would be a good excuse.

Pop took the little boys to help carry and they left early one Sunday morning. They didn't get home until dark, but the truck was full and the little boys were so pooped that they just fell into bed.

There were baskets of every shape and size, so many that they filled a whole corner of our kitchen, and there was a third of a gunny sack of arrowheads. They also brought another sack filled with dried jerky and a haunch of fresh venison that Mom popped in the oven right away just in case a game warden should come snooping around, which they never do. But the best things of all were two fringed deerskin dresses with moccasins to match for Mom and me.

"Your great-grandma says somebody's got to represent the Tutunti tribe," explained Pop. "And she says you're the ones to do it."

The deerskin was as smooth as cream and a lot better looking than a rabbit-fur bib and a bark skirt. I put mine on and it fitted exactly. I could have kissed Great-Grandma Lachance if she'd been there, even though she wouldn't like it.

"Huh," snorted Grandma Longor. "Don't forget you're half Chinook, Plum, even if your Ma ain't."

"Oh, Pop can explain that in his talk," Simon assured her. "And it's good to have both tribes from the reservation."

"Talk? Me?" said Pop quickly. "What talk?"

"Why, you're going to be the master of ceremonies," explained Simon, and we all stared in amazement. It was the first we'd heard about it. "You'll greet the guests and welcome them to the potlatch. Then you'll introduce all of us and explain about the different tribes on the reservation and the customs we brought with us. And then tell about the different dances and the food."

"But I wouldn't know what to say," protested Pop grinning. I could see he was tickled at the idea. "You better do it, Simon. Or Milo, maybe."

"You're the elder," said Simon positively. "And you're the best speaker. Everybody knows that."

Pop didn't argue any more, but after that I noticed he began picking Milo's brains about the stuff he'd dug up on old-time Indians. He even began memorizing Chinook jargon words from a book Milo brought home from the library.

Almost every day Grandma Longor went out to dig roots. The camas was blooming now, and she brought home all she could find. They ought to be wrapped in skunk cabbage leaves and baked underground beneath a hot fire, she told us, and she was really put out when Simon said we couldn't dig up the cement floor of the warehouse to make a fire. She felt better though, when Hank Pierce brought over a silverside salmon, the first of the spring run. She said she'd stew it with wild carrots, moss and some of the camas the way her grandmother used to do.

Milo, who did very neat lettering, made a lot of cardboard signs and we stuck them in grocery store windows from Astoria to Tillamook. They told about the Indian potlatch to be held every Saturday night, starting at 8 o'clock, in Cannon Beach. The poster said authentic dances, stories, real Indian food and curios for sale. The price was $2.50 for adults and $1.75 for children. Simon hadn't intended to charge so much but Perry Schultz talked him into it. He said people always expected to pay high prices at a resort, and anyway it was worth it.

The Cooperville kids who read the signs tried to give me a bad time on the bus, but I pretended not to care. I even made myself smile, after Mildred reminded me, and pretty soon they got tired and stopped.

On the last day of school Mildred told me she had a surprise and that I'd see it at the potlatch Saturday night.

"What kind of surprise? Is it something to do with your costume?" I kind of thought it might be a girdle because she'd been talking about buying one.

Grandma had made her a bark skirt like the rest of us. But when Mildred tried it, with the tight body-shirt, there were a lot of rolls that shouldn't be there. She'd lost over eighteen pounds, too. Grandma thought she looked wonderful and kept telling her so over and over, but Grandma always likes fat people. She thinks I'm too skinny.

"In a way it is," said Mildred mysteriously. "You'll see."

We worked all day Saturday getting things ready at the building. There were big stacks of shells to use as plates, and a pile of small dry firewood that wouldn't make too much smoke. There were buckets of shellfish, standing in cold water so people could start a kitchen midden, which we'd have to gather up afterwards and boil or they'd smell the place up. There was Grandma Longor's rabbit stew to thaw over a hot plate behind a screen, and Great-Grandma's jerky in tough, long strings arranged on a board platter. Hank Pierce had brought another salmon and it had been boned and sliced in strips so people who wanted to could cook it over the fire the way we did the fresh venison. There were baskets of assorted roots that only Grandma knew the names of. Some of them were crisp and nutty, but others were bland, like unscented soap. And there was another basket of wild strawberries that the little boys had picked in the field behind our house. The feather cape was waiting for the proper moment, and Ronnie Wachino thought he was awfully smart because he was going to put on a mask and some jangly beads and be the tyee when people danced with it on.

Perry Schultz was there all Saturday helping us get ready, but Mildred didn't show up. It surprised me a lot because I was sure she'd want to be in on it. I asked Perry if she was sick and he said he was sure she wasn't. He'd stopped by his uncle's and Mildred was fine then. She had been on her way upstairs to wash her hair when he left.

At last everything was ready and we went home to eat supper before we came back. Grandma made two pans of fried bread instead of one, but she wouldn't let us have any. She said it was for the potlatch.

"But Grandma, the old timers didn't eat fried bread," Milo told her.

"They would if they had it," she said crossly. "Everybody likes my fried bread."

"Never mind," said Simon. "It can be the reservation touch."

So we let her take it with her, although Milo kept shaking his head.

By seven o'clock everybody was there but Mildred, and I must say we looked pretty authentic. Anyway, Milo said we did. The men wore their blankets, fastened on one shoulder with a knobby thing that looked like wood but was really plastic, and woven hats that came up to a peak. They had colored bead necklaces, too, and some of shell that Grandma had made. We'd decided not to sell her necklaces because we couldn't find enough shells to make very many. Grandma, Lucy and Sherry wore bark skirts and fur bibs, with their hair hanging down, and honestly they didn't look too bad. And, of course, when she came Mildred would have a bark skirt, too. But I thought Mom and I in our Tutunti dresses looked the best.

By seven thirty I was beginning to worry about Mildred. And then she came. At first I didn't recognize her. She had on her bark skirt and fur bib, but her long blond hair was black!

"Mildred," I called and ran to meet her. Sherry was right on my heels. "What have you done?"

"I dyed my hair." She looked from me to Sherry and back again, and I could see that she'd been crying. "Did you ever see a blond Indian?"

"I saw one once with red hair," said Sherry. "He was part white, though."

"It looks very nice," I said quickly. I was afraid she'd start crying again. "Of course your hair was awfully pretty before, but you can wash this out tomorrow."

"No, I can't," said Mildred. "This is permanent. I thought it would be easier since the potlatch will go on all summer. My folks are awfully mad at me."

"It looks different, and they're just not used to it." I tried to make her feel better, but I didn't blame her parents. Mildred's blond hair had been her best feature.

"I had to do it," she insisted. "Indians don't have blond hair. Not even blood-sister Indians."

A little before eight, Simon told us all to go behind the screens and to keep quiet. There were people at the door, wanting to come in. He and Hank sold tickets and made change, but it was an awful mess.

"We'll have to do something about that," whispered Milo, peeking out from behind the screen. "We ought to have somebody just for the door. Pretty soon Simon and Hank will be busy. They can't take care of people who come late."

"My cousin Perry would do it," said Mildred. "He'd like to." The next minute she had darted out into the audience.

Perry Schultz was sitting in one of the front row benches, and after she whispered to him a minute I saw him get up and go to the door. I'd been wrong in all the things I'd thought about Perrry, and Simon had been right. He wasn't sophisticated and standoffish. He was lonesome and wanted to be included.

After Perry took over the door, things seemed to go better. By that time most of the audience had arrived, and about half the benches were filled. I tried to figure what seventy-five people at $2.50 each would come to, but I couldn't do it in my head. Anyway, some of them were children.

Simon pulled the switch that turned off all the lights except the one over the center. All the benches were in darkness, which was a good thing because I might have been scared if I saw people looking at me. Then, led by Pop, we all paraded out and stood in a line at the back.

"*Klahowya*," said Pop, stepping forward closer to the fire. "Good evening and welcome to our potlatch. My name is Youtl-kut La-lam, which means Long Oar. It was my father's name before me and his father's before him. You whites have shortened it to Longor, but that is not my real name."

I'd never heard Pop talk like that. His voice was deeper than it generally is, and it sounded solemn and strange, the way you'd expect a real Indian to sound, not people like us. The audience stopped rattling their bags of caramel corn and salt water taffy to listen.

Pop went on to tell about the potlatch and what it used to mean, a great feast given by someone to all the others in the tribe. There was always the best food the donor could provide and presents for everybody. Sometimes, when it was over, the man who had provided the potlatch had given away everything he owned.

Pop went on to say that when the Indians were put on the reservation, the coastal tribes were too poor to give presents, but they still had feasts which they called potlatches. And that was what we were going to do tonight. Later on our guests would be able to sample some of the native foods, many of which were unknown to the white men.

Then he introduced us separately as descendants of those who had lived on the Grand Ronde Reservation, and told a little about our ancestors and how great they had been. He said Simon, Lucy and Milo's great-great-grandfather had been the noble Chief Concomely, whom they could read about in history books and that Ronnie's had been Chief Watch-a-no who was the only one in the tribe who could sign for the Clackamas tribe to go on the reservation. When he came to Mom and me, he didn't mention Mom's father, but he really went to town on Great-Grandpa Lachance's grandfather. Pop said he was a French voyageur who worked for the famous Dr. McLoughlin at Fort Vancouver and who had fallen in love with a beautiful Tutunti girl. The only way her father would let her marry would be for the Frenchman to give up his own people and live with hers, and he did because he was so much in love. When he said that, all the ladies in the audience said "Aah!"

None of the old people could remember Hank Pierce's grandfather's Indian name, but that didn't stop Pop. He gave him one. He said that translated from the Chinook it meant Pierce-the-Salmon-With-a-Single-Strike, and that Hank's great-grandfather had been the best fisherman in the tribe. More than once he'd saved his people from starvation in times of famine. As for his own great-grandfather, Long Oar, Pop had a story about him, too, about how he was the best white water boatman of all the Chinooks, and how he had once brought a war canoe with thirty warriors safely home in the face of the greatest storm in the memory of the oldest Indian in the tribe. There wasn't a word of truth in it, but Pop made it sound real, and the people loved it. They clapped and clapped.

When he came to Mildred he said she was a blood sister who had done much for our people and to show our gratitude we had made her one of us. Mildred got as red as the inside of a fresh caught salmon while he was talking, but I could tell how happy she was. She really looked funny with her black dyed hair, but I didn't care. What Pop said was true. She had been good to me, even when I was mean to her, and if I ever heard somebody say anything bad about her again I'd scratch their eyes out.

After that there were the dances, with Pop explaining what they meant. I was glad he did that, because they are a lot alike and unless people know what to look for it's hard to tell them apart.

Then there was something I hadn't known about. Dave Beckett told a story. He sat on the floor before the fire, which somebody had to keep stoking with fresh sticks because we didn't want it to get too big. Pop's booming voice hadn't needed a microphone, but now Perry Schultz stepped out of the crowd and handed one to Simon, who slipped it around Dave's neck.

"I am Chinook," Dave began. "So I can tell story in summer. The Tutuntis of Rogue River tell story only in winter cold. Those foolish Indians say that to tell stories in summer make ears of children grow long; maybe get bit by rattlesnake. Chinook know better. Any time good for story. Tonight I tell how god Kahnie make waves in ocean."

I knew the story so I really didn't have to listen, but when I did I realized that Dave Beckett told it well. I hadn't known he had been one of the storytellers of the tribe. That would have made him an important man. Storytellers were the ones who kept the history of the race. They didn't write it down, but they told it over and over to the people and some of them became storytellers, too. I thought maybe I ought to visit Dave Beckett and see if he knew any stories I hadn't heard. But I'd better do it soon. Grandma had got him to take a bath for this potlatch, but I doubted if he'd do it again.

After that there was the feather cape dance, and I had to admit that Ronnie Wachino did a good job of being the tyee. He gyrated around and made faces while Simon and Hank were dancing, trying to get them excited so they'd trip and drop feathers. Hank lost two and had to pay 25¢ each, but Simon didn't lose any. Then the audience was invited to dance in the feather cape and most of them lost feathers and had to pay the tyee. They seemed to think it was worth it.

After that there was the feast, and you better believe people went for that. A few of them made remarks about the stews, probably because of the moss which gave it a funny taste that I didn't like either, but they really gobbled up the fried bread. Not everybody was brave enough to swallow a mussel, but they all wanted to throw shells on the kitchen midden. Some threw serving dishes as well. We lost a lot that way. They liked salmon cooked over the fire and gnawed on hard jerky and wanted to know where we found the wild strawberries so they could go pick some themselves. Naturally we didn't tell them. The feast ended with smoking the peace pipe filled with kinnikinic, but people weren't too interested in that because by then they had discovered the curio table. Everyone began buying baskets and arrowheads like crazy.

"I told you you should have marked them higher," I heard Perry whisper to Simon.

"Next week we'll raise the price," Simon agreed, grinning.

Finally it was all over. People began leaving and pretty soon we were there all by ourselves, surrounded by broken shells, empty candy sacks and a burned-out fire.

"Well," said Simon. "What do you think?"

"Great!" said Perry Schultz. "It was just great, every bit of it."

Everybody else agreed that it had been a big success. And even I was willing to admit that the first potlatch had turned out better than I had expected.

Next Saturday the potlatch was even better. More tourists came and there were only a few empty seats. Perry Schultz took over the door entirely and the curio table, too. He said if the crowds kept coming we might have to limit the audience to reservations. Simon said that was a good idea and he asked us what we thought about making Perry Schultz our business manager. Everybody agreed, including Perry. The first thing he did was raise the admission price to $3.00 and re-mark all the baskets sky high. It didn't matter. The crowds came anyway, and they still bought baskets.

One Saturday Perry told us that one of the big Portland papers had sent a photographer and a reporter to cover the potlatch. He said he'd known about it a long time but he hadn't told us because it might make us nervous. He wouldn't have told us then only we'd see the flashbulbs on the camera and wonder what was going on.

I don't know if it made the others nervous, but it didn't me. And it didn't Pop. I never heard him talk better than he did that night. His speeches were never quite the same because he made them up as he went along. That night, though, he really went to town. He said the Plains Indians went down because the buffalo were killed, but the fall of the coastal tribes was due to other causes: sickness, brought in by the whites, and the mills and dams built on the river by the settlers which prevented us from using our old fishing grounds.

When the Portland paper came out, it had big headlines "Indians first ecologists. Chief Long Oar of the Chinooks blames water power for annihilation of his race." The story didn't have too much about that, so I guess it was just headlines to sell papers, but it was awfully complimentary to the potlatch. And there was a whole picture page that showed us dancing, and the kitchen midden, and the feather cape dancers, and Dave Beckett telling stories, and everything.

The week after, Perry had to close reservations on Tuesday and was beginning to take them for several weeks ahead. He suggested that we hold a potlatch two nights a week, but nobody wanted to.

One day when I'd driven into Cannon Beach with

Simon, I ran into Mary Beth Perkins and Wendy Carter. I'd walked down to the grocery to pick up some flour for Grandma and they were coming out of the salt water taffy store. There wasn't any way I could avoid them.

"Hello, Plum," said Mary Beth, blocking my path.

"Hello," I said. I tried to get by, but there was a crowd of people milling around and I couldn't.

"I saw your picture in the paper," she said, simpering.

"It was good," added Wendy. "Very good."

"Thanks." All of a sudden I remembered Mildred and made myself smile. They were both awfully dumb because they didn't know it was a put-on smile, and they both smiled back.

"My cousin in Portland was awfully impressed that I knew you," said Mary Beth. "They were down here visiting and tried to get tickets but you were sold out."

"Perry said there's a long waiting list."

"That Perry Schultz!" said Wendy. She closed her eyes and sighed like a sick calf. "I think he's terribly handsome. He looks just like a movie star."

"But he's stuck up," added Mary Beth. "Not at all like his fat cousin Mildred."

That made me mad.

"Mildred Schultz is my very best friend," I said, glaring at them. "I think she's pretty. Did you ever notice her beautiful complexion? There's not a blemish on it." I looked right at a new pimple on Mary Beth's chin and she got what I meant because she turned red.

"I suppose these Saturday night doings keep you pretty busy," said Wendy. She was kind of stupid.

The whole thing had gone right over her head. "I haven't seen you around all summer."

I said they kept me busy.

"But you have to have some time off." Mary Beth wouldn't stay squelched. "My cousin will be back again to visit next month. She's just dying to meet you. Maybe you could come over to my house then."

All of a sudden I wasn't mad any more. They weren't worth being mad at. If the paper hadn't printed our picture and run a long story about the potlatch, they'd have gone on thinking they were better than I was. But the paper had, and now they were trying to pretend we'd always been friends. But we weren't friends. My friend was Mildred Schultz.

"I don't think I could do that," I said. "It would be better if you got tickets to the potlatch. You'll have to reserve them ahead. Mildred and I can meet your cousin then."

The crowd in front of the taffy store had thinned out, so I left. I could feel their eyes staring after me but they weren't laughing.

When I got down to the warehouse, the Deans were just driving up. Mrs. Dean rolled down the window and waved.

"Oh, Plum," she called. "We thought maybe we'd find somebody here. That's why we stopped. If we didn't, we were going up to your house."

"Simon's inside. And Perry Schultz," I told her. "They've got an electrician here. The microphone wasn't working too good Saturday. It kept going on and off when Dave Beckett was telling his story."

Mrs. Dean hopped out of the car, and Mr. Dean

turned off the engine. Today her hair was red, and with her bright green skirt and sweater it made her look like a Christmas postcard. She didn't wait for her husband, but rushed right over and tried to open the locked door. I let her struggle a minute or so before I told her she'd have to go around back.

"Why didn't you say so before?" she said snappishly, and Mr. Dean gave me an apologetic smile behind her back.

We all went around behind where we met the electrician coming out. He must have finished with his wiring.

"Surprise," called Mrs. Dean gaily when she saw Simon and Perry inside.

"Hello, Gloria," said Simon. "Hello, Frank." He introduced them to Perry. Then we all stood around for a minute waiting for somebody else to say something.

"You know, Simon," said Mrs. Dean finally. "I think I've been selfish in making Frank hide his Indian grandparents. After all, they were perfectly good, respectable Indians, peaceful and all that. They didn't go around scalping people. So I thought we'd help you out on your potlatch, both of us. Like I always say, the more the merrier."

"You want to do it, Frank?" asked Simon.

"If Gloria says so." Mr. Dean sounded kind of tired.

"Now, Frank," she said, pouting a little. "You know you're just dying to. You wanted to in the first place, and it was only on account of me that you didn't. I guess you thought it would embarrass me, but it wouldn't, not really. I've got it all worked out. I'll be the white captive and you can be the brave who captured me, and I fell in love with you and stayed with the Indians. I think that might add something to the program, don't you, Simon? Romance is always so appealing."

"I don't believe we'd have time to go into all that, Gloria." I could see a muscle jerking in the side of Simon's face and I knew he was trying not to laugh. "But Frank is certainly entitled to be in the potlatch if he wants. And if you'd like to be his squaw it's okay with me."

I could see that she didn't like the word "squaw," but she couldn't say anything. I could tell she was just dying to be in the potlatch, especially if there was a chance that there'd be another piece in the paper about it.

"I suppose I could put a black rinse on my hair," she said finally, patting all the red curls and puffs. "And I could use a lot of brown makeup. But I think everybody would know I was really white."

"I'm sure they would," he agreed. "But it wouldn't matter since you've married into the tribe. Of course, you'll both have to learn the dances and there'll be rehearsals."

"So long as they don't interfere with my work," said Mr. Dean, sighing. "I got to make a living, you know. Gloria spends a lot of money."

That same week the Wachinos joined the potlatch family. They weren't so silly about it as Mrs. Dean. They just said that after looking at the pictures in the paper and listening to Ronnie talk, they'd decided they were missing a lot of fun. I was glad they'd changed their minds. It was nice to have Nina there.

That left only the Shaws who weren't taking part in it.

Early in August, Simon had to go back to the Veteran's Hospital in Portland for another checkup. I'd been sort of worried about him, and Milo had too. Simon had been taking his pills oftener than he used to, and he hadn't put on any weight since he came home in spite of all the fried bread Grandma was always forcing down him.

I could tell she was worried also because she brewed up a tonic of Oregon grape roots and made him drink some every time she could. Simon said it tasted horrible, but he swallowed a little sometimes just to please her.

This time Perry went in to Portland with him. They went in Perry's sports car, and Simon left his for Mom to drive.

"It's yours till I come back to claim it," he told her. "Drive carefully, and don't worry if we don't come right back."

"You and Perry kick up your heels a little," said Mom. "You've earned it."

Then Simon made a big joke of kissing the little boys and me good-bye. It was awfully funny, because we're not a kissing family, and even when he got back from the hospital he only gave us big hugs. He shook Milo and Pop's hands and said, "Promise you won't get drunk till I see you again," and Pop said "Youtl-kut La-lam never touch white man's firewater." He was more than half-serious, too. Being the master of ceremonies of the potlatch had really changed him. I think it made him feel important again, like he felt when Simon was the football star of Sunset High.

They left on Monday, and we didn't think much about it when they didn't show up on Tuesday or Wednesday. On Thursday we began to look for them, and on Friday when they still weren't home Grandma began to fuss.

"Something gone wrong with my boy," she insisted. "I feel it."

"They'll probably get in tonight," said Milo. His voice was gruff, so I knew he was worried himself. "And Simon's not a boy. He's a grown man."

We were eating supper when we heard the car out front. Andy hopped up from the table and ran into the front room to look out the window.

"It's them," he shouted. "It's Perry's sports car."

"Well, open the door," called Pop. "Help Simon with his suitcase."

We heard Andy open the door and run out on the porch. After a while there were more footsteps, but only Andy and Perry Schultz came into the kitchen. Perry looked tired, as though he hadn't slept for a long time, and his clothes were rumpled and he needed a shave.

"Simon didn't come," said Andy in a puzzled tone. "Perry says he's not coming."

"No," said Perry. "Not any more. But the last thing he told me to tell you was that he expected the potlatch to go on tomorrow night without him."

Grandma began to cry in a funny way I'd never heard before, and Pop pushed back his chair and stood up.

"Where is he?" he demanded. "Where's Simon?"

"He's—" Perry swallowed hard. Then he reached in his pocket and pulled out a folded piece of paper. "He sent you this. I guess it will explain."

Pop took the paper, opened it and squinted at it. Then he handed it to me. He never got very far in school and he hates to read anything for fear there will be long words in it that he doesn't know.

"You read it, Plum," he said. "Read it aloud so we can all hear."

It was in Simon's handwriting, and somehow I managed to read it all before I broke down and began to cry.

DEAR FAMILY AND TRIBESMEN,

By the time you read this, Kahnie will have taken me into the next world. I don't want you to grieve. I want you to be happy that we had these last few months together. The doctors told me it was going to happen. They could do nothing more for me, so they let me leave the hospital to spend the time with you. Kahnie has let me stay longer than the doctors thought possible. I think it was because he wanted us to have the potlatch. Don't let it die just because my body is no longer there. I will be there in spirit. Go on with it. Show the world that you are proud of what you are.

My heart is full of love for you all,

SIMON

I don't know how we ever got through the potlatch the next night, but because it was the last thing Simon asked of us, we did. The audience probably thought, after looking at us, that all those stories whites tell about the Indian being stoical are true. Nobody, except maybe Gloria Dean, smiled, but the people didn't know the difference. I heard them telling each other afterwards how interesting and educational it had been.

Perry came over to our house the next day, and Mildred came with him. I was glad she did. She didn't say anything. She only gave me a squeeze, but it made me feel better to have her there.

Simon had told Perry what was going to happen when they drove in to Portland together. He'd planned exactly what he wanted done. He wanted to be cremated, which seemed strange at first, but it didn't after you thought about it, because he wanted the ashes taken out to the bar of the Columbia and scattered there. In the old days, before the white men, the Chinooks put their dead in canoes on Memaloose Island or on scaffolding along the river. When the winter storms came along, the high tides washed the canoes out to sea. Simon wanted to go back to sea, too, and it was the only way he could do it.

On Tuesday, the men took the day off and everybody went to Astoria. All our family went, of course, and all the Wachinos and Dave Beckett and Perry and Mildred Schultz. The Deans and the Shaws were to meet us there, along with Lucy's family. Perry didn't show up until just before we were ready to leave home and who should be in his sports car but Great-Grandma and Grandpa Lachance. Nobody else had remembered them, but Mildred had, and when she told her cousin he left before daybreak to go after them.

The Lachances took up all the room in Perry's car so Mildred rode with us. I wondered if Great-Grandma kept crying and moaning the way Grandma Longor did all the way down the highway. I felt sorry for Perry if she did. Mom whispered that it was called keening and was the way the old Indian women mourned, but it certainly didn't make anyone feel any better to hear her.

At Astoria our friends were waiting on the dock.

Hank Pierce was already in his fishing boat and he started up the engine when he saw us coming. Pop got out of the truck, carrying the little box that held all that was left of Simon, and got into the boat. We watched it till we couldn't see it any more.

The Lachances stayed overnight with us, and for once Grandma Longor and Great-Grandma got along fine. They both moaned and cried, and finally Grandma went outside and came back with a bucket of wood ashes from the stove that Andy had carried outside yesterday. When she saw them Great-Grandma let out a shriek, then they both dived into the bucket and began smearing ashes on their heads.

I'd been feeling terrible about Simon, but for some reason that struck me as funny and I began to laugh. The little boys were laughing, too, and I could see Mom's mouth twitching as though she wanted to.

"I wish Simon could see this," said Milo. "He'd never believe it."

Great-Grandma Lachance and Grandma Longor keened even louder. They beat their chests and rubbed ashes in their clothes.

"Stop it, you two!" yelled Pop suddenly. His face was red and I could tell he was really mad.

"Why they stop?" asked Great-Grandpa Lachance. "They act proper."

"They've mourned enough," shouted Pop. "Simon wouldn't want them to carry on that way, and I don't neither. Simon said in his letter not to grieve. He said to carry on like he was still here. And that's what I intend for us to do."

Great-Grandma snorted and Grandma sniffed, but

at least they stopped keening. One thing about the old Indians, a man had the final word.

After that it was Pop who kept the potlatch going. He made the framework for a sweat bath hut and Grandma covered it with skins and rushes so Pop could explain about how the old Indians used to fill it with steam from hot rocks and water to drive out sickness. "The Chinook sauna," he called it.

"Don't know why you went to the bother," grumbled Grandma. "Potlatch's only got a little while to go."

"There's always next year," Pop pointed out.

The Shaws had joined us by this time. I liked the way they did it. That day in Astoria Mr. Shaw had told Pop that now the potlatch was one man short and while he couldn't pretend to take Simon's place, he and his family would be honored to take part in it.

The funny thing about the potlatch was that our feelings had changed. In the beginning, some of us had been in it just to please Simon. It wasn't that way any more. We were doing it for ourselves. We didn't even think too much about the audience any more, except that we hoped to prove something to them. And the thing we hoped to prove was that we weren't second-class citizens, we were Indians, Oregon Indians, and just as important as the Sioux or Cheyenne or any of those tribes you hear so much about.

When Pop told the story about spearing the whale, I was as proud as though I'd been there paddling one of the canoes. And when we did the dances, I kept thinking of the thousands of people who had danced them before I was born. They were old dances, older than the fox trot, or the jitterbug, or the white man's waltz. Each one of them meant something, and when I went through the steps I held my shoulders high and danced proudly. I think the others felt that way, too, because there wasn't the joking and laughing that there had been before. It was our heritage, and we were proud of it.

Our last potlatch was on Labor Day weekend. Everybody was doing his best, as though we were all performing for Simon. And I've never heard the audience applaud so loud.

Mary Beth's family had finally got tickets and they were there with their cousin from Portland. Mary Beth brought her up to me afterwards. She was a scrawny girl with acne.

"How did you ever get to be in it?" she asked, staring at Mildred.

"Because she's a blood sister of the tribe," I said quickly.

Mildred's hair was growing out blond at the roots and she'd got tired of dieting and was putting on weight again. I saw the girl stare at her curiously.

"It takes a very special person to be a blood sister," I said. "Indians have an extra sense. We can tell when a person's beautiful inside, and Mildred is."

"Oh," said Mary Beth and her cousin respectfully. I saw Mildred look at me in a funny way and I knew I'd have to explain that Indians didn't really have an extra sense, and that I'd just said that to put the two in their places.

Perry had asked us to stay after the audience had left to talk about the money we'd made. We hadn't been dividing it up every week. Instead he'd put it in the bank for us. While we were waiting, Ronnie Wachino got me in a corner.

"Hey, what's the matter with you, Plum?" he said. "I thought we were friends. But you've been treating me like I had the plague."

"Why would you want to be friends with a kid?" I asked him scornfully. "So you can lead her around by the nose?"

"I didn't call you a kid!"

"You certainly did. The day you took me for a ride on your Honda."

"Well, maybe you were then." Ronnie's face began to turn red. It started in his neck and went up. "But you've grown since." It was a poor excuse, but I suppose it was all he could come up with on such short notice.

"Besides, we don't believe in the same things," I continued. "You're a revolutionary. I'm not."

"Who said I was a revolutionary?" His face was really red by this time, and I wondered if I'd gone too far. After all, I didn't want him to get too mad at me.

"The way you talked that day sounded like it. You wanted to overthrow things."

"Then I was wrong. This way is better," he said quickly. "People are really looking at us now. They know we're here. They think we're something else. Your brother Simon was smart when he got this idea."

"Yes, he was." I decided I might as well forgive him.

After all, he was the best looking boy I knew and there would be a carnival at Sunset High next year. I smiled my very nicest smile, and he smiled back.

"Friends?" he asked, putting out his hand.

"Friends," I agreed. He had a nice warm handshake.

When all the audience had gone Perry locked the door. Then he pulled out a bankbook.

"I've kept very careful records," he said. "I'll be glad to show anyone who is interested. But to put it briefly, after expenses, you have $3,795.75. Some of you have been in this longer than others. How do you want to split it up?"

Everybody gasped. We had no idea we'd made so much. Then Mr. Wachino spoke up.

"Some of us have been kicking this around," he said. "And we think it would be a fine thing to put this into a scholarship for Indian kids. The Simon Longor Scholarship. What do the rest of you think?"

I glanced at Milo. His eyes were starey and his nose was doing a rabbit twitch. I knew what he was thinking.

"Does it have to be just this year's high school graduates?" I asked. "Or could it maybe be from a few years back?"

"Heck no," said Mr. Wachino. "Anybody who wants can apply, so long as he has Indian blood. And the one who deserves it most will win. Might even have two scholarships if there's enough money. What do you all say?"

And everybody shouted, "Yes!"